He loved the sight of her.

Her gray eyes were darker than storm clouds, her cheeks flushed. As she ranted, all Lauren's righteous indignation drove out the defeat he'd been feeling after the incident with Wyatt. Drew not only liked this warrior side of her, he needed it. Needed her strength.

Catching him staring, she stopped her tirade. "Sorry. Got carried away, I guess. I'm just not putting up with anyone scaring Wyatt. The boy's been through enough."

Her mama lioness instincts reared up, making him want to be in her protective circle along with the boy. Not that he needed protecting—it was just great having someone care enough.

"You are terrifying," he told her.

Her chin rose. "Are you making fun of me?"

He grinned. "No, I'm not. I'm admiring you."

What are you doing? an inner voice asked him. *You don't deserve her.*

Why not? he asked himself. But he knew the answer.

Because if he started believing he deserved her, he'd give his whole heart away.

And what if she didn't want it?

Jill Kemerer writes novels with love, humor and faith. Besides spoiling her mini dachshund and keeping up with her busy kids, Jill reads stacks of books, lives for her morning coffee and gushes over fluffy animals. She resides in Ohio with her husband and two children. Jill loves connecting with readers, so please visit her website, jillkemerer.com, or contact her at PO Box 2802, Whitehouse, OH 43571.

Books by Jill Kemerer

Love Inspired

Hometown Hero's Redemption

Jill Kemerer

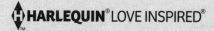

HARLEQUIN® LOVE INSPIRED®

Recycling programs for this product may not exist in your area.

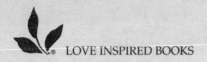

LOVE INSPIRED BOOKS

ISBN-13: 978-0-373-62283-2

Hometown Hero's Redemption

www.Harlequin.com

Printed in U.S.A.

Therefore encourage one another and
build each other up, just as in fact you are doing.
—*1 Thessalonians* 5:11

Thank you to the Waterville Fire Department for your bravery and sacrifice. We are blessed by your heroism. Special thanks to Steven Brubaker for answering my endless list of questions so patiently. Any errors in the book are mine!

Finally, thank you to all the men and women who dedicate their lives to keeping us safe. Jason Kernstock, we couldn't be prouder of you!

Chapter One

Ice cream fixed a lot of problems, but it wasn't going to fix this.

Drew Gannon passed a chocolate-brownie sundae to Wyatt. The tiny ice-cream shop had two tables inside and a patio full of picnic tables out front. Not much had changed in the fourteen years he'd been gone. If his best friend, Chase McGill, hadn't insisted, Drew never would have moved back to Lake Endwell, Michigan. But Wyatt, Chase's ten-year-old son, deserved a stable life away from the public eye. Drew had promised Chase he'd give Wyatt that life. He just needed to convince Lauren Pierce to help him.

Drew handed a twenty to the teen behind the counter, turned to Wyatt and pointed to the glass door leading to the patio. "Why don't you head outside and save us a picnic table—the one with the striped umbrella."

Wyatt nodded. He was far too grim for a little boy. *Poor kid.* The past nine months had traumatized him, and Drew was doing the best he could to make his life normal again. Well, as normal as it could be given the circumstances. A murdered mom. His dad in jail for trying to avenge her death. What a horrible situation.

Drew tried to spot Lauren. Would he recognize her after all these years? The only women he could see were either too old or not old enough. What if she'd changed her mind about meeting him? He wouldn't blame her. If their situations were reversed, he'd probably never want to speak to her again.

"Here you go." The girl shoved the change in his hand. "Napkins are over there."

He thanked her, inserted a straw into his orange slushie and strolled to the door, pushing it open with his shoulder. An early-May breeze guaranteed sweatshirt weather. The sunshine highlighted Wyatt's scrawny, slumped shoulders. His gaze seemed glued to the wooden table. Drew doubted he'd touched the ice cream.

Maybe he should call Lauren. Grovel if necessary.

"What's wrong with your sundae?" He playfully punched Wyatt's arm. "Don't tell me you suddenly hate chocolate."

His hazel eyes opened wide, as if he'd been lost in his own little world, which, Drew guessed, was exactly where he'd been for the past several months.

"I'm not hungry." Wyatt slowly swirled the spoon in the gooey mixture, but he didn't eat any of it.

Drew took a drink of slushie to ease the helplessness lining his throat. Would the kid ever enjoy simple pleasures again?

He checked his phone to see if Lauren had texted or left a message. Nothing. He needed someone to stay with Wyatt when he worked overnight at the fire station, and not just anyone would do. According to Drew's mom, Lauren had the credentials—years of working with neglected children and a degree as a social worker—as well as the time. Apparently, she'd quit her job in Chicago and moved back to Lake Endwell a few months ago.

When he'd called Lauren last week, her clipped words had made it as clear as a freshly cleaned window she wanted nothing to do with him. She hadn't relented after he'd tried to explain Wyatt's situation, either. He'd finally resorted to pleading with her to just meet him in person before saying no. His words could never convince her the way one look at Wyatt could.

Except he hadn't mentioned Wyatt joining them.

Manipulative? Yes.

Necessary? Absolutely.

The thud of a car door jolted him from his thoughts. He glanced ahead and his mouth dropped open.

Lauren Pierce.

Still had that long, wavy blond hair. She didn't head to the door of the ice-cream shop—no, she strode directly to the patio. A baby blue hoodie was zipped halfway up over her white tank top. Her enormous light gray eyes captured him. A film reel of memories flashed through his mind so quickly he couldn't keep up.

Breathtaking. A woman who stopped men in their tracks.

Why had he been such an idiot back then?

Something had changed, though. Her nothing-gets-me-down smile had been replaced with something else. Something familiar.

Drew darted a glance at Wyatt.

If he hadn't lived with Wyatt's diminished personality for months, he might not have recognized it. Lauren had been traumatized, too. And he wanted to know why. The captain of the cheerleading squad had had everything going for her. She'd never let anything shake her optimistic spirit.

"Glad to see you again. You're looking good." He rose and held his hand out. She ignored it, arching her eyebrows instead. Why had he said that? It was something the old him would have rolled out. Heat climbed up his neck. The last impression he wanted to give her was that he was the same old Drew.

"So when did you get back?" Lauren asked as she sat opposite them.

"Yesterday. Wyatt and I are renting a cabin on the lake. Used to be Claire Sheffield's—well, Claire Hamilton now. Remember her? Her brother, Sam, was living next door, but Claire said Sam, his wife and their little boy moved to a house just outside town, leaving both cottages empty. Anyway, we've made a dent in the unpacking." Drew's knee bounced rapidly. He was babbling, and Lauren gave no indication she was up for small talk. He'd better get right to it. "This is Wyatt. Chase's son."

A flicker of kindness lightened her eyes. "Nice to meet you."

Drew elbowed Wyatt, who belatedly said, "Hi," and dropped his attention back to the table. This was going great.

"Thanks for coming." He didn't blame her if she left, but to his surprise, she stayed. She looked weary—but stunning all the same. "Mom told me you moved back in January. You're a social worker?"

"I did move back, but no." She shook her head, her demeanor icy. "I used to be a social worker. I don't do that anymore."

Hmm... He hadn't considered she no longer wanted to work in her field. "Mom said you had a temp job."

"I do. It's great." She nodded, and her smile appeared

forced. She addressed Wyatt. "What do you think of Lake Endwell so far?"

One shoulder lifted in a shrug.

Drew's knee bounced double time. "We'll have to rent a boat or borrow a canoe or something soon. Wyatt here—"

"I don't want to canoe," Wyatt said.

He put his arm around Wyatt. "You'll change your mind. Summer is the best season to enjoy the lake."

"I know a little bit about your situation, Wyatt." Her voice was low, soothing. Wyatt's gaze locked with hers. "It's okay."

"Everyone knows." Wyatt hung his head. "I guess you saw the pictures. Those guys were always sneaking around with their cameras. The whole world knows."

"After a while, no one will care." Compassion glowed from her eyes.

Drew squeezed Wyatt's arm. "No reporters will take your picture here. That's why we moved. We're going to have a nice, quiet, normal life until…you move back in with your dad."

Wyatt didn't say anything, but he studied Lauren, which Drew took as a good sign. In high school, she had always seemed to be an open book. Straight-A student, prom queen, crusader against teen drinking and, of course, the captain of the cheerleading squad. And since he'd been the star quarterback, everyone had assumed they would make the perfect couple.

Not even close. They'd never dated. Not once.

Drew cleared his throat and leaned in. "So why did you move back?"

"I didn't want to move, but I needed a change. And my family is here."

"I didn't want to move here, either. I want to go home," Wyatt said. "Can't we go back to Detroit?"

That made three of them not wanting to move back to Lake Endwell. Drew would have cracked a joke if the atmosphere wasn't so tense.

"What's in Detroit?" A trio of emotions sped across Lauren's face—sympathy, sadness and wariness.

Wyatt hauled in a breath, his face full of animation for the first time in forever; then the joy slid away and he sighed, defeated. "Nothing, I guess."

"There must be something." Her voice lilted, coaxing Wyatt to talk, but silence won. "Never mind. You don't have to answer. We all have things we'd prefer no one knew about."

"My dad," Wyatt whispered. "But he's in jail."

"My dad was in jail most of my life," Lauren said. "He died a few years ago."

Drew straightened. Why was she lying? Her dad had never been in jail. Bill Pierce was one of the most upstanding men the community had ever seen, and he was definitely still alive.

"Really?" Wyatt sounded skeptical and hopeful at the same time. "What did he do?"

"He murdered two men." She rubbed her arm, not looking him in the eye.

"Oh." He dropped his attention to the uneaten sundae melting into a puddle of brown and white. "But you're so pretty."

She laughed. "Thank you. I'm not sure that what I look like has anything to do with it, though."

"Sorry." Wyatt blushed. "I just meant… I guess I don't know what I meant."

"I think I do." She scrunched her nose. "People who

look like they have it all together have problems, too. Big problems. Like yours."

He seemed to chew on the thought. Drew dug his nails into his jeans. Maybe he'd been all wrong about Lauren. Was she fabricating a sob story to make Wyatt trust her?

"Would you do me a favor, Wyatt?" Lauren asked. "Go inside and buy me a chocolate ice cream. In a cup, please." She handed him a five-dollar bill. "If you don't mind?"

He took the money. "You want sprinkles?"

"No, thanks."

Drew waited until Wyatt was safely indoors before he turned back to Lauren. "Why did you lie to him?"

"I didn't." Those clear gray eyes held nothing but truth.

"But Bill—"

"Bill isn't my real dad. I was adopted."

"What do you mean, you were adopted?"

She shrugged. "Adopted. As in my parents adopted me."

Of course she hadn't lied. Relief spread through his chest, releasing the tension building inside. "Look, I need a babysitter. An adult to stay with him when I'm working at the fire station. Mom moved to Arizona last year or I'd ask her. I'll be on twenty-four hours and off forty-eight, so it's not every day. And I think we both know that not anyone will do in this situation."

She was already shaking her head. "I don't think so."

"Why not?"

"I'm not the right person." She pushed her hands against the table as if preparing to leave.

"You're exactly the right person." Her brittle expression reminded him to be gentle. "Look, I'm sorry. I don't blame you if you hold a grudge, but I'm not the same guy I was. I've changed. And you don't owe me anything except maybe a slap in the head or a kick in the rear, but I'm not asking this for me."

He let her see the sincerity in his eyes. Didn't move. And he prayed. *Lord, please don't hold my foolishness and arrogance against me. Wyatt needs her. I feel it deep down in my gut.*

She shook her head, and he clenched his jaw, trying to come up with something that would convince her. She'd been the most honest, upright person he'd ever met. Someone who would be a good influence on Wyatt.

He didn't deserve someone like that. But Wyatt did.

"I can't be there for him every hour," Drew said. "I need to rely on someone I can trust. Someone with experience dealing with the kind of trauma he's lived through. I wish my mom could help out, but she's on the other side of the country. She told me you're the one for Wyatt, and, frankly, Mom's always right."

"I'll give you the number of a nice college student I know. He'd probably stay with Wyatt."

"Or you could keep the guy's number and make this easy on everyone."

She tilted her chin up. "I don't think you understand. My life is on hold."

"What?" He tried to figure out what she was talking about but came up blank.

"I'm not the person for the job."

Lauren watched as Drew processed her words. He was even better-looking now than he'd been in high school, if such a thing was possible. And a firefighter? Forget putting out the fires. More like igniting them. He could be the cover model for any fireman calendar.

Stupid hormones. Must be playing tricks on her. She'd never been attracted to him before. Not much, anyway.

Maybe a tad.

A person's soul should match their appearance, and he didn't have the integrity to round out the package.

She probably wasn't being fair. The man in front of her seemed the polar opposite of the boy she'd gone to high school with. Back then he'd been a cocky jerk. It hadn't been enough he'd been the most popular guy at Lake Endwell High—oh, no—he'd been the most popular guy in the whole town. Everyone had loved him. As the big-time quarterback, he'd taken the football team to two state championships. College coaches had scouted him for months. Parents had adored him. The town had revered him.

And she'd loathed him.

He and his friends had made it their mission to mock her. She had never been Lauren Pierce to them. She was "the prude," "Miss Perfect," "do-gooder" and, her personal favorite, "Prim Pierce." They'd invited her to parties where there was beer, knowing full well she didn't drink. Their girlfriends—always the most inappropriately dressed girls in school—looked down on her. The guys teased her for her modest clothes and made lewd comments about her bare legs when she wore her cheerleading uniform.

They'd made her feel like a leper the first two years of high school. By the time junior year had rolled around, her confidence had kicked in. She'd prayed for them, and their taunts might as well have bounced off a shield, because they'd no longer bothered her. In fact, she'd felt sorry for Drew and his crew.

"Are you getting married or something?"

She barked out a laugh. "No, nothing like that."

"Then I think you *are* the person." He tapped the table twice with his knuckles.

"You don't know anything about me." *Oops*. She'd let bitterness creep into her tone. *Oh, well*. Bitterness had crept into every cell of her body since last December. She'd failed Treyvon and Jay. Would she ever fall asleep at night without seeing their trusting faces?

"You're right." He ran his hand through his short, almost black hair. "But I know you have integrity and devoted your life to helping others. Back in school, I had an ego as long as the Mississippi and as deep as the Grand Canyon. I never thought about anyone but myself. I apologize for that. And I apologize for—"

"Look, we don't have time for unnecessary apologies. Wyatt will be back soon. I want to help you out, but I can't. I *was* a social worker, but I don't work with troubled kids anymore."

"What will it take for you to say yes?"

"Nothing." She lifted her hands, palms up. "I give you credit for using your best weapon—Wyatt—to try to seal the deal, but no."

His nostrils flared. "Do you have another job?"

"Yes."

"Permanent?"

Ugh. He knew. Always knew people's weak spots.

"I'm filling in at LE Fitness for Laney Mills. Maternity leave. She'll be back next week."

"There you go. The timing's perfect. You need a job. I need help. I'll pay you whatever you're making there, plus ten percent."

She fought irritation. This relentlessness was part of Drew's personality, part of what had made him a winning football player. But, for real, the man needed to accept the word *no*. She didn't owe him anything. "You can find someone else."

"He needs *you*."

That threw her off. Drew didn't know her, not really. "How can you say that with a straight face?"

"Look, he's been through a nightmare I wouldn't wish on anyone, and he's hurting. Withdrawn. I'm worried he'll never be the same fun kid I've spent so much time with over the past ten years. I'm all he has."

A nightmare... For eight years she'd worked with kids embroiled in nightmares. Chicago's inner city had supplied a lifetime of them. She'd thought she could help. She'd been wrong. But Wyatt's face when he'd admitted there was nothing for him in Detroit scratched at her heart. She knew exactly how he felt.

There'd been nothing for her anywhere the first seven years of her life.

Drew squared his shoulders. "I could find a babysitter or someone else with children where he can stay on my overnights, but he's been through too much. You know how to handle kids like him. Know what he needs. I want someone who will come to our house. I want him to sleep in the same bed every night. Feel safe. Grow up as normal as possible."

Kind of like the normal life her adoptive parents gave her. *Uh-oh.* He'd twisted the screw into her vulnerable spot.

"Even you have to admit he needs special care right now. He lost his mom. His dad's in jail. He's scared of photographers jumping out of the bushes. Please, Lauren."

Yes was on the tip of her tongue, but the memory of last December's phone call haunted her. "I can't help. When I say I can't, I mean I really can't. Even if I agreed,

I'd only be giving you false hope he'll be okay. He's not an easy fix, Drew."

He opened his mouth to counter, but Wyatt came back, setting the ice cream and the change in front of Lauren.

"Thank you, Wyatt." She smiled at him. Skinny with light brown hair and one of those cute faces destined to grow up handsome. She couldn't halt the longing in her heart to help him. To take him under her wing and just let him be a kid. Help him adjust to life without his parents.

She'd had the same longing every day since she was sixteen years old. She'd thought she was meant to help kids like Wyatt—kids like her—ones with broken wings and matching spirits. But her efforts were for nothing. Worse than nothing. She'd given those two boys hope, and look where they'd ended up.

How had she been so wrong about her life? Her calling?

Her neck felt as though a noose was tightening around it. "Well, I'd better get going."

"But you didn't eat your ice cream," Wyatt said.

She tried to smile, but his hazel eyes held a glimmer she recognized. It was a sliver of need, asking her if he was worth anything. *Yes, Wyatt. You're worth everything, but I'm not the one who can help you.*

"I guess we're even, then." She pointed to his bowl. He blinked, and the glimmer vanished. Guilt compressed her chest until she could barely breathe. She darted a glance at Drew and wished she hadn't. He looked unhappy.

Without a word, Wyatt pivoted and jogged away. Drew followed him.

The guilt squeezing her chest so tightly exploded.

She'd made the sweet kid feel unwanted, and she *did* want to help him. Wanted to get to know him, to hear all about his little-boy day. She wanted him to know his parents had made bad choices, and none of it was his fault. She wanted to be part of his recovery.

But she wasn't recovered herself.

One broken soul couldn't fix another.

Lauren watched Drew draw near the boy. He crouched to his level and put his hand on his shoulder. The picture they presented radiated love. It didn't take a degree in psychology to see Drew would do whatever was necessary to keep the boy safe and make him happy.

For the briefest moment, she wanted the same. For Drew to chase her and do whatever it took to keep her safe and make her happy.

Which proved how messed up she was.

She'd had her life planned out since she was sixteen. Devote her life to neglected kids, eventually get married, have a family of her own. That was the funny thing about life. Plans changed. Not always for the better.

Now what? She had no plan. Temporary jobs didn't fulfill her. She wanted a new life purpose. Something to dig into. Something to make her feel alive again.

In the distance Drew rose and kept his arm around Wyatt. He pointed to a black truck. While Wyatt trudged to the passenger door, Drew marched back to her.

"That was my fault," he said, head high. "I took a chance bringing you two together, and it blew up in my face. I'm sorry. But I'm still asking you to consider it. Don't decide now. Give it a few days. I'll call you."

Please don't.

He strode, tall and confident, back to the truck.

She grabbed the ice-cream containers and threw

them in the trash. Drew didn't need her. He thought he did, but Wyatt would be better off with someone else.

Anyone else.

For months she'd avoided thinking about her next move, but this meeting drove home the fact that she needed a long-term plan. A new career. A way to get out of this nothingness she'd been in. But what?

Drew Gannon was dangerous. He tempted her with the one forbidden fruit she'd promised herself she'd never take a bite out of again. Her purpose no longer included helping kids with hard lives. Not even ones who wiggled into her heart and made her want to feel again. Not even Wyatt.

"See how I'm holding the rod? You want to bring it back like this, then flick it forward while you hold the reel's button." At the end of the dock in front of their cabin, Drew demonstrated a perfect cast.

After leaving JJ's Ice Cream, he'd driven to the elementary school to sign papers for Wyatt's enrollment. The kid hadn't said a word since they'd gotten home an hour ago. Wyatt held a fishing rod in his hand, but he'd yet to attempt to cast a line. "Try it."

With a loud sigh, Wyatt laid the pole on the dock and slouched in one of the camping chairs Drew had brought down. He stuffed his hands into his sweatshirt pockets and stared out at the sparkling blue water.

Drew was ready to pull his hair out. Today had been bad. Really bad. What had made him think springing Wyatt on Lauren would help his cause with her? He shouldn't have badgered her. Shouldn't have expected her to help him out, not after the way he'd treated her years ago. Not only had it backfired big-time, but he was no closer to finding a babysitter than before. Unless the college kid she mentioned… No. He didn't want anyone but her.

Did Lauren still have the same impression of him from way back when?

What did it matter?

If he could just figure out how to get through to Wyatt. He'd always been a big part of the kid's life. Chase's career as a wide receiver kept him training and traveling nine months of the year, so Drew had helped take care of Wyatt off and on during football season. Wyatt's drug-addicted mom had never been around. Even if she had been, she certainly couldn't have taken care of him.

"Don't you want to show off your fishing skills when your dad gets out?" Drew kept his tone light. Chase made mistakes—big mistakes—but Drew believed in him and hoped Wyatt would, too.

"Six years from now." Wyatt kicked at the dock with his sneaker.

"His lawyer said he'll get out in three if he models good behavior."

Wyatt looked up at Drew. "Do you think he'll do it? Get out early?"

Drew lowered himself into the chair next to him, ruffling Wyatt's hair with his free hand. "Yeah, I do. He'll do anything to be back with you. He loves you."

Wyatt's face fell again.

"What did you think of Lauren?" Drew asked.

He shrugged.

"We went to high school together. I wasn't very nice to her."

"Is that why she left without eating her ice cream?"

"Maybe she wasn't hungry." Drew cranked his line in a little ways. "I don't think she left because she held a grudge. Like I said, I was mean to her in high school, but she was probably the nicest person I knew. Very genuine."

"Why were you mean?"

Drew kept one eye on the bobber out in the lake. "I was stupid. When I was fourteen, I had a crush on her. One of my friends told me she'd never go out with me. He said she was too perfect. I asked one of the other cheerleaders if she thought I had a chance with Lauren, and she laughed. She told me Lauren would never date me, that she thought she was better than everyone. I took their word for it. And my pride made me say things and treat Lauren in ways I regret."

"She deserved it if she thought she was better than you."

"No, she didn't. No one does." Drew shook his head. "I trusted people who didn't have my best interest at heart. I should have asked Lauren myself, instead of listening to my so-called friends."

"What do you mean?" Wyatt's face twisted in confusion.

"Looking back, I think every guy in my class had a crush on Lauren."

"She's pretty."

"Yeah, and some of the cheerleaders were jealous of her."

"Oh."

"They had their own reasons for not wanting me to ask her out. Lauren kept to herself, but it didn't mean she was stuck-up. I hope you think about that as you get older. Don't believe everything you hear."

"Like about my mom." Wyatt got a lost look on his face again.

Whenever Drew tried to talk to him about his mother,

Wyatt's mouth shut tighter than a vacuum-packed seal. Maybe this was the opening he needed. "What about your mom?"

"Forget it."

"Why don't you tell me?"

"People said things."

"People say a lot of things."

Wyatt's sad eyes met his. "They said she was on drugs and owed that Len guy money, and that's why he killed her."

Drew reeled in the rest of his line as he tried to figure out the best way to respond. Missy and Chase had never married. They were together for only a few years before Missy left and got mixed up with drugs. "You and I both know she went to rehab last year and was trying hard to live a healthy lifestyle."

"Yeah. I was glad when she moved by us. We'd play games with Dad and go to movies."

"Your dad cared about her. They were even talking about getting back together."

Wyatt nodded, the corners of his mouth drooping. "Do you think she was in a lot of pain before she died?"

While he was glad Wyatt was finally talking, it hurt to think he had to have his conversation. No kid should have to deal with this. A murdered mom? A dad in jail? Wyatt deserved an intact family—didn't every kid?

"No. The police said she died quickly."

"Do you think she's in heaven?"

He squirmed. This was another one of those tricky areas. Drew had no idea what Missy had believed. "The Bible says as long as you trust in Jesus as your savior, you go to heaven."

"But what if she didn't?"

"I wish I could tell you your mom is in heaven. I hope she is, but I don't really know. What do you think?"

"I want her to be."

"Me, too."

Wyatt grabbed his fishing rod and stood at the end of the dock. "How do I do this again?"

Drew showed him the steps. Wyatt's first attempts didn't get the line far, but after a few more tries, he cast it out several feet. Drew gave him a high five.

"Hey, Wyatt, we're going to be all right." He put his arm around him. "I hope you know that."

"Do you think Lauren would stay with me while you're at work?"

Drew's chest expanded. The kid liked her. Wyatt had already opened up more in the last ten minutes than he had since Chase went to jail three months ago. But Lauren didn't work with troubled kids anymore. She'd made that clear. What had happened in Chicago to make her quit?

"I don't know." This conversation alone hammered it home—Wyatt was dealing with much more than the average kid. He didn't need a college student around to watch TV and heat up chicken nuggets. He needed to make sense of his shattered family. He needed Lauren. She might not believe she could help him, but Drew knew she could.

And maybe in the process, he could help her, too. Her sunny smile had grown cloudy since he'd last seen her, and he wanted to bring her joy back.

He'd just have to figure out how to get her to say yes.

Chapter Two

"I've been talking to Stan, and we think you should offer a class."

Lauren looked up from her computer screen at the reception desk of LE Fitness the following afternoon. Megan Fellows, one of the Zumba instructors, stood in front of her. Since moving back in January, Lauren had reconnected with Megan, two years her junior, and they'd become good friends, partly because Megan was so upbeat and made it her mission to not let Lauren dissolve into a puddle of depression. What would she think of Drew's offer?

It didn't matter. Lauren had made her decision. She needed to stay strong and say *no* when Drew called. If he called…

He would call. His take-charge personality assured her he would not let this matter fade away.

"What kind of class?" Lauren typed in a new client's information.

"A tumbling class for cheerleaders."

A tumbling class? The idea didn't horrify her. "I don't know."

"You keep saying you're figuring things out, but you

don't have a plan." Megan's brown ponytail bounced as she drummed her fingernails on the counter. "And Laney will be back on Monday. What are you going to do?"

The million-dollar question. She had no idea. Megan was right about her not having a plan—every time she tried to figure out her next step, she froze. It was difficult letting go of the dream she'd had for most of her life. She couldn't handle the heartbreak of social work, but she still liked kids. Tumbling classes might be something to consider.

"I don't want you to go all hermit-like in your apartment again." Megan rested her elbows on the counter. Her face had the concerned look that poked at Lauren's conscience.

"Well, I *have* been offered a babysitting job."

"Babysitting?" Megan grimaced. "What ages are we talking? Three? Five?"

"Ten. Do you remember Drew Gannon?"

"Do I remember Drew Gannon?" Megan rounded the counter in a flash and took a seat next to Lauren. "Tall, built and studly? Oh, I remember."

"That's him." Lauren had probably been the only girl in school who hadn't drooled all over Drew.

"I've had a crush on him since I was in second grade. I know he's a little older than me, but how could a girl *not* like him?"

"Every girl in this town liked him at one point or another." Lauren straightened the papers on the desk. "He's back. Hired in at the fire station. He's taking care of his best friend's son."

"Why?" Megan's screwed-up face almost made Lauren laugh.

"I'm not getting into all the gory details, but Wyatt will be living with him for several years."

"A single dad. Maybe he needs some help...from yours truly."

Lauren swatted at her arm and laughed. "I'm sure once word gets out he's back in town, there will be plenty of willing female bodies at his door."

"He's single, then?"

"Seems to be."

"So how do you fit into all this?"

"His schedule," Lauren said. "Twenty-four hours on. Forty-eight off. He needs someone to stay with Wyatt while he's at work."

Megan pressed her index finger to her lips. "Why you?"

"My degree. Experience. His mom recommended me."

"Please tell me you jumped at the chance?"

She shook her head. "I can't, Megan. You know I can't."

"I know no such thing. You can. And you should."

"Uh, no. I'm not putting myself through it. No more emotionally damaged kids. My heart can't take it. I'm finally getting back to normal." If normal included not sleeping well, avoiding any public event and refusing to date any of the men brave enough to ask her out since she'd moved back...

Her new normal sounded sad. Add a few more felines, and she could be a reclusive cat lady.

"You love kids. And this is only one kid. It would be perfect. You wouldn't be trying to find him a foster home or visiting him at a crack house. You'd be heating SpaghettiOs and helping with math problems. Easy." Megan snapped her fingers.

Megan always made things sound easy. Unfortunately, Lauren knew better. There were so many factors making the situation impossible. Like the fact that Drew had been a complete jerk to her for years. Sure, he'd seemed caring with Wyatt and had apologized yesterday, but it didn't guarantee he was a stand-up guy.

And then there was Wyatt. Withdrawn, emotionally shattered—it was written all over him. She couldn't be simply a babysitter. She didn't have it in her. No matter how much she told herself not to grow attached, not to fall in love with the kids, she did. She'd love him. And she'd get hurt. If she took care of Wyatt and made a bad decision, it could send him back to square one.

"You want to say yes," Megan said. "I can see it in your eyes."

"He was so skinny and small and withdrawn. He was sweet, too. I felt an instant connection."

Megan smiled slyly. "And did you feel the connection with his temporary dad?"

Oh, yeah. When she agreed to meet Drew, she'd been sure she wouldn't find him attractive at all. His personality in high school had made him unattractive to her. But watching him interact with Wyatt? Seeing the way he pushed and pushed for Wyatt's sake?

Made him enticing.

"Um, I guess a little bit. I mean, I have a pulse, and he looks like…"

"A hot fireman."

"Yeah." Lauren glanced up as someone headed her way. *Phew.* Saved by the shift change. "I'm out of here."

"I think you should go for it," Megan said. Lauren grabbed her purse out of the drawer, ignoring her. "If not, consider the tumbling class."

She gave Megan a backward wave and walked out,

soaking in the afternoon sunshine. Why was she still thinking about Drew's offer? She wasn't changing her mind. She'd made her choice.

She drove to her apartment over the hardware store on Main Street. Maybe Megan was on to something with the tumbling class. Lake Endwell High used to have an elite cheerleading program, but it had been several years since they had won any competitions. Tumbling classes would help, but not enough to get the program back on top.

What Lake Endwell needed was a boost to its cheer-leading program.

Cheer academies had popped up all over Chicago while she lived there. One of the foster moms she knew owned one, and Lauren had visited it several times. The students came from surrounding school districts, and they traveled all over the country for competitions. Most of them went on to cheer in high school.

She parked in the lot behind her building. Years of gymnastics and cheerleading qualified her, but she hadn't choreographed in a long time. And own a business? She wouldn't know where to begin. While making her way to the back door, she checked her phone for messages.

Drew stood near the entrance. "I called the fitness place, and Megan Fellows told me you just left. She said I could find you here."

I'll get you back for this, Megan. She plastered a smile on, ignoring the way her heartbeat stampeded at the sight of him. "What can I do for you?"

"I feel bad about yesterday. Let me buy you a cup of coffee."

"No need to feel bad or buy me coffee. We're good. Your conscience can be clear." She tried to push past him, but his broad shoulders blocked the door. He wore loose-fitting jeans and a dark gray pullover. By the strained look on his face, she'd say she annoyed him. *Good.*

"Will you please hear me out?" The words were soft, low. She let out a loud sigh.

"This isn't necessary. I hold no ill will against you. I hope you have a wonderful life." *Without me in it.*

"You were never good at lying." The side of his mouth quirked up, and challenge glinted from his brown eyes.

"You're right. I'm not." Hiking her purse over her shoulder, she tipped her chin up. "I like Wyatt. I'm tempted to help you because of him. But I never worshipped you like the rest of this town did, and I don't plan on it now. So go ahead and demand your way, but you won't get it—not from me. All you have to do is walk three steps and you'll find someone else who's more than willing to do whatever you ask."

He scowled. Maybe she'd gone too far. She hadn't seen him in years, and it wasn't his fault her life fell apart, so why was she taking her anger out on him?

And why was she so angry, anyhow? She'd been keeping it together reasonably well for months.

"I don't want anyone to worship me. I'm just a guy. Someone who messed up most of my life." Drew crossed his arms over his chest. "I admire you for being straight with me. Don't worry—I'll leave you alone."

"Wait." She caught his arm. His muscle flexed under her hand. She swiftly pulled back. "I guess one cup of coffee wouldn't kill me. I know you're trying to help Wyatt."

"The Daily Donut?"

She shook her head. "Closes at two. Have you been out and about yet since moving back?"

"No, why?"

Tapping her chin, she realized he had no idea what was about to hit him. "Then let's skip the coffee and go to City Park."

"Isn't there another coffeehouse in town?"

"You're missing the point. When word hits around here you moved back, you're going to be bombarded."

He grimaced. Had he paled? "City Park it is."

Drew Gannon, scared? She'd never thought he could surprise her, but never was a long time. Why wouldn't Mr. Hometown Hero have made the rounds when he arrived?

"Give me a minute to drop off my purse." Maybe a little chat in City Park wasn't such a bad idea after all.

Drew strode next to Lauren along the sidewalk. If he was going to have any chance at getting her to help Wyatt, he needed to show her he'd changed. This would probably be his only shot. She smelled fresh, the exact same way she looked. He'd always thought she belonged on a California beach. All-American, pure sunshine.

But the sunshine had sharpened to lightning over the years—she certainly hadn't held back with her opinion a minute ago. The way she'd put him in his place had shocked him at first. But, oddly enough, he liked her even more because of it.

He'd dated too many women who had their own agendas. He couldn't remember any of them saying exactly what was on their minds.

How long had it been since he'd been on a date?

Five years? Six?

"Where's Wyatt, by the way?" She easily kept pace with him.

"School. His first day. I'm picking him up at three thirty."

"School already? You don't waste time, do you?"

"I wasted enough time when I was younger. I don't see the point in waiting when something has to be done."

"What do you mean?" They reached the last store on the street. A quarter mile and they'd be at the park.

"You know how I was in high school?" He didn't glance at her, not wanting to see how she viewed him. He could guess well enough. "I thought I was somebody. Didn't work hard at anything but football, and by senior year I wasn't even giving that my all. I believed my hype. Thought I was special."

"Well, everyone around here agreed, so you probably were." Her dry tone made his lips twitch.

Keep it serious. Show her you mean this.

"I was unprepared for college. I actually thought the coaches were going to fawn over me the way it was here, not that you would know what I mean…"

"I know what you mean."

"Yeah. I guess you would, but I had no clue. I got to college and was a nobody. Third-string quarterback. For the first time in my life, everyone around me was as talented—more talented—than I was."

"I hope you don't expect me to feel sorry for you."

He shot her a look. There was the megawatt smile he'd missed. He chuckled.

"I had it coming. I struggled at practices, and instead of working harder and giving it my all, I complained about the coaches. Told everyone they didn't like me. That I deserved to be a starter." He gestured to the park entrance, and they headed toward the gazebo. "Do you know how many snaps I took in games?"

She made a face and shrugged. "None?"

"Two." He almost shuddered. "None would have been better. I threw two interceptions. The sum total of my freshman year stats. Two plays. Two interceptions. I gained weight, lost muscle, didn't attend a team meeting. And I was so dumb, I was actually shocked— and I mean shocked—when I was cut from the team. No more scholarship. No more college."

"I'm sorry, Drew. I didn't know all that."

"Well, you're the only one from this town who didn't. I have my doubts about moving back."

She hopped up on a picnic table and perched on the top, facing the water. Seagulls landed in the distance, and two ladies power walked on the bike trail. The unmistakable smell of the lake filled the air.

"Why did you come back?" Lauren pushed her hair to the side of her neck. The LE Fitness lime-green T-shirt she wore under a black formfitting warm-up jacket hugged her slender body. He liked the way it looked on her.

"Chase asked me to. He wanted Wyatt to grow up in a healthier environment, away from the reporters and the private school full of kids with wealthy parents. He always joked I was the most normal person he knew. He wanted normalcy for Wyatt."

"You? Normal? Debatable." She leaned back, resting her hands on the table, and grinned. Understanding knitted between them. The peace of the lapping waves nearby mellowed his senses.

"You gave me the ten-second version on the phone, but what really happened to Wyatt's mom? And how did you become his guardian?" Lauren crossed one leg over the other and faced him.

"It's kind of a long story."

She propped her elbow on her knee. "I've got all afternoon."

"Don't say I didn't warn you." *Where to start?* "Chase and I met in college. We were roommates. We had a lot in common, liked the football lifestyle. The girls, the parties, the accolades."

She snorted. He opened his hands as if to say, *This is what you get.*

"Chase was more grounded than I was. The guy was pure talent. And he worked his tail off to be the best. I can't tell you how many times I wished I would have followed his example."

"Yet he's in jail, and here you are." The words were barely audible.

"True. Anyway, he's my best friend. I refused to come back to Lake Endwell after getting kicked out of college. And even if I could have afforded out-of-state tuition, I had no desire to continue. I was bitter. Worked at a gas station, shared an apartment with a group of potheads. I couldn't face life without football. Couldn't face my parents. Certainly couldn't face my old buddies from home."

"Some of them would have been supportive. There are some good people here."

"You're probably right, but I couldn't handle it. I'd gone from being the hero to a nobody. Chase was the one who kept me going for two years. He told me I was better than that. Helped me realize I could do something with my life besides football. He fronted the money for me to take classes to be a firefighter and an EMT. A few years later I decided to continue my training and become a paramedic. It was brutal. I almost quit. Chase didn't let me."

"Sounds like a great guy."

"He is." Drew leaned forward, his clasped hands dangling between his knees. "He met Missy while I was working at the gas station. She was gorgeous, and she liked to party. That was all Chase looked for in a girl. At the time it was all I looked for, too. They fought a lot, but they'd make up just as quickly. She got pregnant his junior year. Moved to Chicago with him when he got drafted. They never married. She left when Wyatt was two, taking him with her, and the next year Chase was traded and moved to Detroit."

"Did she move, too?"

"No. Not then, anyway. If she would have, things might not have spiraled out of control the way they did. She found a new boyfriend, Len, who also became her drug supplier. When Chase realized how addicted she'd become, he fought for full custody of Wyatt—and he won. From that point on, I was a big part of Wyatt's life."

"How so?"

"I'd gotten a job in Dearborn the year before. When Chase gained custody of Wyatt, I transferred to a fire station closer to them. He was on the road or training for over half the year. He hired a part-time babysitter, but I stayed at his house whenever he was traveling. I had my own apartment the rest of the time. Wyatt has no living grandparents. That's why the courts appointed me to be Wyatt's guardian."

"So you've been helping take care of Wyatt for years?" She tilted her head.

"When Chase couldn't."

"That's actually a good situation for Wyatt. He's

comfortable with you and doesn't have to learn a new routine."

"Living here will be a new routine for us both. I hope his first day is going okay."

"I do, too. Kids make friends easy at his age. I'm sure he'll fit right in."

Drew gazed out at the water. "I don't know. He's too quiet. And he never used to be shy."

"Losing your parents will do that to you." She rubbed her upper arms although it wasn't cold. "You still haven't told me what happened."

He hated discussing it. It wasn't as if he hadn't memorized the details. Once he opened his mouth, he knew he'd be able to tell her the facts in a detached voice. If only his insides wouldn't twist and cry out at the senselessness of it all. Missy hadn't deserved to die, and his best friend shouldn't be in jail.

"Over a year ago, Missy went to rehab and, once out, decided a change of scene would help her stay clean. She moved to Detroit to be in Wyatt's life. She and Chase reconnected, were even dating again. On a hot day in August, Len showed up at her apartment. They fought. He choked her to death." He cleared his throat to dislodge the lump forming. "It changed Chase. He became obsessed when Len skipped bail. He hired a private investigator, and when they located Len, he went there to confront him. No one knows exactly what happened, but Chase drove over Len with his truck."

"He didn't kill him, though?"

"Broke his leg." He rubbed his chin. "Chase was found guilty of second-degree attempted murder. Len is serving a life sentence in prison for first-degree murder."

Drew glanced at Lauren to see her reaction. "Is that the saddest story you've ever heard?"

She shook her head. "No. It's not."

"That's pretty heartless."

"Is it?" She stood, shaking her legs out. "Work in the inner city of Chicago for eight years. You'll see worse."

He rose, too, shoving his hands in his pockets. Logically he knew awful things happened every day all over the world, but they hadn't touched him the way Chase and Missy did. His own line of work put him face-to-face with horror on an ongoing basis. While he cared about the people he helped who had been in accidents and fires, he didn't love them the way he did his friends, so their tragedies didn't feel as devastating. He probably should feel guilty about that, but he didn't.

"Let's go walk along the lake." He took her by the elbow, directing her to the lakeside path. "Tell me about Chicago."

She strolled beside him. "I'm trying to forget."

"What do you want to forget?"

"It's kind of hard to forget if I talk about it." She acted lighthearted, but the tiny furrow in her forehead revealed the truth. Whatever had happened must have affected her deeply.

"You got me there." He wouldn't push her.

"Yeah, well my do-gooding days are over."

He cringed, remembering the way he and his friends had taunted her. How she'd walk down the school halls with her spine so straight it looked like it would snap. They'd thought she was stuck-up, but he knew better now. She'd been protecting herself from them.

Why had he been so clueless? So thoughtless? So mean?

"I hope that's not true," he said. "The world needs more people like you."

She snorted. "Not even close. I was so naive. Thought I could make a difference. I tried. I really did try."

"I'm sure you made a big difference in a lot of people's lives."

She quickened her pace, and he sped to keep up with her. "I'd get kids placed in a foster home, and the next month they'd be removed at the foster parents' request. They needed stability, but did they get it? Or I'd try to get kids out of an unhealthy, neglect-filled home, but the parent would find a way to work the system."

"Some of the cases you worked on must have turned out well."

"Some did. The last one, though... I couldn't do it anymore. Those kids meant too much to me. I always got in too deep emotionally."

"It's better to be emotionally invested than to be apathetic. When you don't care about other people, you only really care about yourself. Trust me. I know."

"What if you don't care about yourself, either?" The breeze blew the hair around her face, and she tucked it back behind her ear.

"Then you end up living with a bunch of potheads and working at a gas station because you're so mad at the world, you can't handle living in it." He checked his watch. "I didn't realize the time. I hate to cut this short, but I've got to pick up Wyatt."

"No problem." They turned around and started walking back to her apartment. "Do you ever miss playing football?"

"Miss it? I still play."

"When?" Skepticism laced her tone.

"Me and the guys throw the ball around whenever possible. You should see us when football season starts. We watch all the college and NFL games, and we split into teams to play outside, too. Well, we did back in Detroit, anyway."

Her smile lit her face. "So I assume you'll be coaching a rec team for Wyatt this August, huh?"

"Unfortunately, no. Chase made me promise I wouldn't let Wyatt play."

"Why not? Isn't he the big football star?"

"That's part of the problem. He blames the celebrity lifestyle for coloring his decisions. Like I said, he wants Wyatt—"

"To have a normal life."

"Yep."

They crossed the street at a traffic light.

"Hmm…" She appeared deep in thought.

"What's the 'hmm' for?"

"I guess I was thinking no one really has a normal life."

Drew opened his mouth to refute it, but she had a point. What was normal?

His job was normal. He loved being a firefighter. Craved the adrenaline rush of his duties. Didn't mind the danger.

Lauren's complexity intrigued him. What about that last case had made her lose her faith in herself? What had her life been like in Chicago? Why did this golden girl, who seemed to have it all together, not view herself the way he—and everyone else—did?

The questions would have to wait. They reached the parking lot, and he stopped in front of her building's back door. "Thanks."

"For what?"

"For giving me the time of day. For letting me talk to you."

A blush spread across her cheeks. *Whoa.* He couldn't help staring at her and wishing things were different.

"Listen, I'm taking Wyatt to the fish fry at Uncle

Joe's Restaurant Friday night. Why don't you join us? Say, six thirty?"

She bit the corner of her lower lip and averted her gaze. "I'll think about it."

At least she hadn't said no. It would have to be enough. "You know where the restaurant is?"

"Everyone knows where Uncle Joe's is."

He nodded and jogged to his truck. As he started it up, he looked back, but she'd disappeared inside.

For a firefighter, he wasn't being smart. He knew better than to light matches near a dry forest. What was he doing, thinking about beautiful Lauren Pierce? He ran his palm over his cheek. Just because he'd made peace with his past didn't change the fact that he'd made big mistakes.

She'd been too good for him then, and she was too good for him now.

One thing had changed, though. She'd grown sassy enough to tell him off.

Maybe this was life's funny way of getting back at him. Because that sass only made him like her even more.

Lauren didn't bother changing out of her work clothes after Drew drove away. Instead, she poured a glass of sun tea, selected an adult alternative radio station to play over the wireless speaker on her shelf and stretched out on the couch. What was she going to do now? Babysitting Wyatt no longer felt like an absolute no. But what about the tumbling class or researching a cheerleading academy? Wouldn't either be the smarter move?

Zingo, her Maine coon cat, jumped on her stomach. "Oof. Watch it, big guy." He circled on top of her legs three times before curling into a purring ball. She reached down to pet him. "Love you, too."

Staring at the ceiling, she tried to empty her mind, but it churned with all the things Drew had told her. About Wyatt. About himself.

Hearing about Wyatt's parents hadn't shocked her, and she sniffed at how Drew thought it was the saddest story. Yes, it was sad, but so was the destruction she'd witnessed over and over in her life.

Physical abuse, parents giving drugs to their small children, molestation, death—it horrified her. She'd dealt with it all, seen it all, and she wished Wyatt could have been spared. At least he had been able to rely on Drew all this time.

A laugh escaped her lips, and she clapped her hand over her mouth. Where had that thought come from? In one day she'd flipped from thinking Drew a complete waste of time to an upstanding guy?

He'd been honest. Open. Bared his soul, not knowing if she'd retaliate or not.

She was surprised she hadn't. Well, she kind of had. Her angry outburst earlier had come out of nowhere. The venom still puzzled her.

What had Drew said about being mad at the world? She closed her eyes, trying to remember. They'd been discussing her getting too close to the kids, and he'd said something—something important.

Being so mad at the world you couldn't handle living in it. That was what it was.

She sat up. Zingo glared at her in protest, then resettled on her lap. Mindlessly, she stroked his fur.

Was that why she couldn't move forward?

Was she so mad at the world she couldn't handle living in it?

No. She shook her head. *Of course not.* She wasn't angry. She was protecting herself from a job that wasn't good for her anymore.

She could move forward. She *would* move forward. The idea of helping the local cheerleaders had sparked something inside that had been dormant since high school. "Sorry, baby, but I have to get up." She cradled the huge gray tiger-striped cat and kissed his head before setting him back on the couch.

She'd call Angela Duke, the foster mom who owned the cheerleading academy in Chicago, and find out what was involved with starting her own. She hoped she still had Angela's number. Where had she put the files with her Chicago contacts?

Rummaging through her bedroom closet, she found a box of old purses, a bag stuffed with receipts from the past five years, stacks of books, a jar full of change and two suitcases. Three boxes sat on the top shelf, so she located her step stool and dragged them down.

One looked like the box where she'd thrown the file with her personal contacts. She pawed through it. Appliance manuals. Why did she keep them? She tossed one over her shoulder, unearthed an old trophy and kept digging.

The purple duffel bag.

She dropped it like it was covered in battery acid. Taking two steps back, she fell to her knees.

A home movie of her earliest memories played through her mind, stealing her breath, stinging the backs of her eyes.

She'd kept the dirty, ripped purple duffel bag packed with every one of her belongings from the time she was three years old until she was eight. She'd been living with the Pierces for more than a year before she finally believed they were her forever family.

Creeping forward, she took it in her hands and held it to her chest. Emotions rushed through her. Remembering the fear of being placed in a new foster home. Five different homes in four years. Some had been good, others not so good, but none had lasted.

She'd been unwanted.

The purple duffel bag had been the only thing she'd owned. Every night before she went to bed, she'd fold her clothes and zip them into it.

Always ready. Always prepared to move.

One of the boys at the third home tried to steal it from her, and she'd grown blind with rage. Six years old. Already too street-smart for the world. That night she'd snuck into the kitchen, grabbed a paring knife, went into his room and waved the knife, demanding he give it back.

He had.

And she had been placed in a different home two weeks later.

The look in Wyatt's eyes yesterday, the one questioning if he was worth anything, roared back. Wyatt hadn't lost all his hope yet. Not the way she had so early on. And he wasn't living in a hovel with his meth-addicted mom on a notorious gang's street like Treyvon and Jay had been.

Drew thought she'd be good for Wyatt.

She clutched the bag tightly and almost laughed. He had no idea that six-year-old Lauren had threatened a kid with a knife to get this bag back. Her nicknames had been "Prude" and "Do-Gooder" and "Prim Pierce," and they were so far from the truth, it was laughable.

She wasn't a wild, angry little girl anymore. Her

adoptive parents had given her more than a home. They'd given her faith in a loving God. They'd given her a baptism, a new person to replace the old, rotten, unwanted one.

And she'd promised herself she would be worthy of their love, and she'd help kids like her, the way they had.

She uncurled her legs, set the duffel bag on top of the box and sat on the edge of her bed.

Lord, I've been avoiding the hard prayers lately, the ones where I ask You to show me Your will. I was afraid—I am afraid—You'll ask me to do something I can't handle.

Could she babysit Wyatt and not have her heart broken?

Who would help Wyatt if she didn't?

At least he had Drew.

The longing she'd sensed in Drew before he left earlier had drawn her heart, unbidden, to him. He'd given her a peek of who he'd become, and she had to admit, time and experience had turned his drive into something less selfish than it had been in high school.

Could she say the same about herself?

She'd consider meeting him and Wyatt at Uncle Joe's Restaurant Friday night. In the meantime, she'd find the Chicago file.

Chapter Three

"Hope you're ready for the tastiest fish fry you've ever eaten." Drew glanced over at Wyatt next to him in the truck Friday night. Daylight was sticking around longer—a nice change from the short winter days behind them. He wondered if Lauren would join them tonight.

"I hate fish."

"Well, you're going to love this fish. It's covered in batter and deep-fried. Ask for double the tartar sauce. Just a tip from me to you."

Was that an eye roll? Drew grinned. An eye roll was better than dead silence. At least the kid was showing signs of life. He'd been subdued, shrugging and grunting yesterday when Drew asked him about school. Drew had met with his teacher earlier, and she'd assured him Wyatt, though quiet, was settling in fine.

He wasn't so sure.

If Lauren didn't show up tonight, he would take it as a sign he needed to find another babysitter. In fact, he should find someone else, no matter what. After she'd told him about leaving Chicago and not being able to handle the emotional pain of her cases anymore, he understood. It would be unfair to ask her to help, know-ing she was still upset about whatever had made her quit her job.

What *had* made her quit her job?

The parking lot was ahead. The building must have been remodeled. It looked bigger, newer than it had when he was in high school. One thing that hadn't changed? It was packed.

All his peppiness about the fish fry wasn't fooling his roiling stomach. This was the first time Drew would be out in public, and he dreaded what was coming. How did people greet a fallen hometown hero? He supposed he was about to find out.

Parking the truck, he studied the entrance. Did any of his old friends still live around here? Would they treat him the same? He hoped not. He wasn't the same. Didn't ever want to be that guy again.

"Aren't we going in?" Wyatt asked.

"Yeah. Let's go."

Drew said a silent prayer as they crossed the lot. *Lord, whatever happens, help me take it like a man in there.*

"Hey, Uncle Drew, isn't that Lauren?" Wyatt tugged on the sleeve of his shirt.

Just hearing her name flooded him with relief. There she was—long blond hair waving down her back. Her jeans, bubblegum-pink T-shirt and athletic shoes made him smile. She couldn't have been prettier in a ball gown.

"Lauren," Drew called. She turned, a smile spread-ing across her face when she spotted them. She waited near the door until they joined her.

"So, Wyatt, is it okay if I sit with you two?" Her eyes twinkled.

Wyatt's tongue must have frozen because all he seemed able to do was nod.

"Good to see you." Drew opened the door for her.

She entered the restaurant. "Let's find a table."

Drew stopped at the hostess station. The girl behind the stand held a stack of menus. "It's a thirty-minute wait inside, but we have a few tables open on the deck."

He looked at Lauren. "Do you want to eat outside, or is it too cold for you?"

"Outside is fine. It's a beautiful night. What do you think, Wyatt?"

Wyatt was eyeing the fish and deer heads mounted on the pine walls.

"Wyatt," Drew said.

He flushed. "Huh?"

"Do you want to eat outside?"

He peered at the crowd. Large windows displayed views of the lake. "Yeah, sure."

They weaved through the tables on their way to the patio doors. Drew didn't look left or right. He concentrated on following Lauren's graceful movements.

"Gannon?" A voice boomed over the lively conversation. "Gannon the Cannon?" The man leaped out of his chair and stood between Drew and Lauren. Wyatt instinctively huddled closer to Drew. He kept his arm around the kid's shoulders.

"It's me, Mike Schneider. Man, I haven't seen you in ages. How've you been?" Mike clapped him on the back, his face beaming.

Drew's inner serenity crumbled faster than a week-old cookie. Mike Schneider had been a linebacker on the team, one of the guys he ran around with. Someone who had thought he was above getting in trouble. The same way Drew had been.

"Good to see you, Mike." He nodded, hoping to bypass the reunion and get to the deck ASAP.

"So what brings you to town? You visiting?"

"I'm actually moving back. I start at the fire station next week. You still live here?"

"Just visiting my folks with my wife—you remember Tori?" He pointed to the corner of the table, where Tori waved above several empty beer glasses. Another vaguely familiar couple sat across from her. "My sister, Paige, joined us. This is her husband, Brent."

"Good to see you, Drew. You're looking good." Tori winked. He gave her a tight nod. Tori James had flirted with Drew throughout high school and, if his memory served him correctly, had never had a nice thing to say about Lauren. The same way he hadn't.

The ladies began to whisper as Mike continued. "Hey, remember sneaking out to the Flats with Brittany? Man, did we have fun. Late-night swimming has never been the same."

Shame lit a bonfire in his gut. Drew stepped forward. "Yeah, well, we're holding up traffic."

Mike ran a calculating gaze across Drew over to Lauren, and his eyes about bugged out. "Am I seeing things or what? Is that Prim—"

"It's Lauren Pierce." Drew frowned. Lauren's face was a polite mask—nothing was getting through it.

"What? Are you two together?" Mike chortled as if it was the funniest thing he'd ever heard. "Is this your kid?"

"This is my godson, Wyatt. Good to see you." Drew clenched his jaw and propelled Wyatt forward. His veins felt like they were going to explode. Every table they passed seemed to be staring, pointing and whispering, but maybe it was his imagination. The patio doors were merely a few yards away.

"What's wrong, Uncle Drew?" Wyatt rubbed his biceps as soon as Drew let go when they made it to the deck.

"Nothing."

"Are you mad?" Wyatt sounded worried.

"I'm fine." Drew studied the people seated outside but thankfully didn't see anyone familiar.

Lauren led them to the most secluded table. She patted the chair next to hers and smiled at Wyatt. "Drew hasn't been home in years."

Wyatt didn't look convinced. He began to nervously chew his fingernail. "Let's go home."

What was bothering him? He'd been okay when they had arrived.

"Do you want to go home?" Lauren asked, her voice calm and reassuring.

"I don't know."

His face looked pale. Drew ticked through possible reasons Wyatt had gone from excited to jittery so quickly. Was he getting sick?

"Are you sure you're not mad, Uncle Drew?"

"I'm not mad," Drew said. "Like Lauren said, it's been a long time since I've been here, and I guess I'm nervous."

Lauren tapped Wyatt's arm and pointed to the lake. "The water is so shimmery tonight, and, look, there's a duck and her babies." Slowly Wyatt's color returned, and he seemed to relax. A waitress stopped by for their orders, and a family came outside with a young girl and a boy about Wyatt's age.

"Hey, Wyatt." The boy waved and sped over to their

table. "I didn't know you were coming tonight. Want to go try to win a prize with the claw?"

Yearning and fear collided in Wyatt's expression. Drew hitched his chin. "Go ahead. I thought I saw the claw machine inside those doors. You can see us from there."

"I'd better stay here." Wyatt shrank into himself.

Lauren smiled at the other boy. "Why don't you pull up a seat? You two can talk a bit and play on the claw machine a little later if you feel like it."

"Okay, let me tell Mom and Dad." The boy ran off.

Wyatt straightened, clearly happy with her solution. A round of Cokes arrived, and the kid returned, taking the seat next to Wyatt.

"I'm Wyatt's uncle Drew, by the way. What's your name?"

"Hunter."

"Nice to meet you, Hunter."

The kid had already turned away and was asking Wyatt about a video game. His enthusiasm must have been contagious because soon Wyatt couldn't stop talking about the world he was building, whatever that meant. Drew guessed it had something to do with his new video game.

Now that Wyatt was occupied, Drew could focus on Lauren. He'd been waiting all day, wondering if their conversation Wednesday had changed her mind about him. She'd been less prickly when he'd told her about life after football, but she'd had time to process it all since then. He wouldn't blame her if she didn't want to be around him. Especially not when Mike had just reminded her Drew had been such a jerk before.

He'd just have to show her he'd changed. For good. "I'm glad you came tonight."

"Me, too." The low sun at her back made her hair glow. "I want you to know I'm not—"

"Drew! We thought that was you!" Two attractive women squealed, prancing to their table. His stomach plummeted. Shelby Lattimer and Beth Jones. They'd been on the dance squad in high school, and he'd dated both. Not at the same time, of course.

"Well, look who's here." Beth narrowed her eyes at Lauren. Beth wore painted-on dark jeans, a tiny black shirt and sky-high heels. Drew raised his eyebrows at the too-revealing outfit. "Haven't seen you anywhere but the fitness center since you moved back, Lauren. You're finally hitting the town, huh?"

"Hey, Drew." Shelby's long brown hair was pulled into a low ponytail, and she twirled a section in her fingers. Her outfit, a tight red dress and stiletto boots, also left little to the imagination.

"Beth, Shelby." The glint in Lauren's eyes was the only crack in her composure. "Didn't see you at spin class Monday night."

"Yeah, I had a date." Beth's gaze flitted to Drew, and she smiled suggestively. "Just casual, though."

Drew almost choked at the way Lauren's lips pursed.

More people joined Beth and Shelby, all talking at once to Drew and Lauren. There were a lot of shoulder slaps and references to football. There were a few veiled sneers. He couldn't make sense of most of it, just kept nodding and repeating, "Yeah, it's good to see you," and keeping an eye on Lauren, who handled the questions thrown her way with ease.

The waitress arrived with hot platters of food, and the crowd dispersed. His mind tumbled with impressions. The night had just begun, and dealing with all these people from his past already exhausted him. What could Lauren possibly think about this? She probably thought he loved all the attention. High school Drew would have loved it.

"Well, Wyatt, dig in." Drew waved his fork at Wyatt's plate. He craved the anonymity of the previous years, wanted nothing more than to go home, sit on the couch and watch TV the rest of the night, but tonight wasn't about him. "Best fish you'll ever eat."

"I ordered chicken tenders," Wyatt replied in a deadpan voice. Hunter, still sitting next to him, snickered. Wyatt offered a piece of chicken to Hunter, who happily accepted it.

Lauren lifted her Coke to the boys. "To the best chicken tenders you'll ever eat."

They exchanged curious glances.

"You're supposed to clink your glasses with mine," she whispered. They brightened with understanding and lifted their Cokes. "Cheers."

Drew sighed. Lauren was so good with Wyatt. But she'd already told him she wasn't babysitting. This entire night hammered home why he'd been delusional. His past was messy, and he didn't want to drag her back to those hurtful days.

He might as well forget the whole thing. He'd find another babysitter and wouldn't force his way into her life.

"Can I have some quarters?" Wyatt and Hunter stood next to Drew with their palms cupped. "You're right. I can see the claw machine through the window."

Lauren wanted to pull both boys into a hug and kiss their foreheads and assure Wyatt Drew wasn't going anywhere. He'd be right there, where Wyatt could see him. She set her napkin on her plate and watched in amusement as Drew unfolded his wallet and handed Wyatt a five-dollar bill.

"Go up to the front desk and they'll give you change," Drew said. "Come back if you need anything."

The boys ran off. Lauren noted that Wyatt looked back three times as if he were certain Drew would vanish at any moment.

"He's scared for you." Lauren turned back to Drew. "Afraid you'll be gone like his mom and dad."

The stunned expression on Drew's face cleared. "That's crazy. I'll never leave him."

"He probably thought the same about his parents." Lauren pushed her plate away. "I think that's why he wanted to go home earlier. He sensed the tension when you were talking to Mike."

"Tension is normal." Drew shifted back in his seat. She didn't recognize the expression in his eyes, and she was good at reading people. If she had to guess, she'd say it was regret.

"He's on high alert. Dealing with a lot of new developments in his life. Tension isn't normal for him, not now, anyway."

"I'll have to hide it then." He wiped his hand down his cheek. He had the look of a man in way over his head. The actions she'd witnessed the few times they'd been together said otherwise. He was good at this— good at handling Wyatt. He just didn't know it.

"I didn't mean to imply… You don't have to hide anything." Lauren bit her lower lip to keep from saying too much. She'd been close to a decision about babysitting, and everything she'd seen tonight—from Drew's obvious discomfort with Mike and Tori to the kind way he'd greeted everyone who stopped by the table without encouraging them to reminisce about the good old days—showed her he'd changed.

He'd told her football had been the only thing he'd cared about in high school. Well, his single-mindedness had shifted. The man would do anything to protect Wyatt and give him a good life.

She would help them. Who else would take care of Wyatt when Drew was at the station?

Beth? Shelby?

Over her dead body. No, Drew was right. Wyatt needed someone who understood what he was going through.

Wyatt needed her. At least until he started feeling at home here. The summer should give her plenty of time to make him comfortable in this town. Then he'd be equipped to get through his days like other children. And when Angela Duke called her back, she'd research the cheer academy. If it seemed to be way over her head, she'd teach a tumbling class and find another office job this fall.

Lauren folded her hands and straightened her shoulders. "I'll babysit."

"What?" His jaw dropped; then he closed his mouth and swallowed. "I thought you said—"

"I changed my mind."

He steepled his long fingers. "I don't know. After what you told me about getting hurt and leaving Chicago, I'm not sure it's best for you."

"Are you saying you don't want me to babysit anymore?" She had never considered she'd actually convinced him she wasn't a good fit for Wyatt.

"Lauren, I would like nothing more than for you to take care of Wyatt. You're way more in touch with his emotions… I feel like a dummy compared to you."

Could her heart smile? Drew looked adorable when he was complimenting her and unsure of himself.

But he wasn't unsure of himself. He'd been born sure of himself.

He also had this idea she was perfect, and she'd be the easy solution to making Wyatt's life all better. She couldn't even figure out her own. And perfect? What a laughable concept. When Drew realized she was a mess, would he send her packing?

The purple duffel bag flashed in her mind.

"Are you sure you want to?" Drew tilted his neck to the side, and his expression—so raw, so apologetic—tossed cold water on her doubts. She was being silly. They were grown-ups. And this was about Wyatt.

"Yes." She nodded decisively. "But only until the end of the summer. He'll have made enough friends by then you'll have no problem finding someplace he can stay when you're at work. And, please, keep your expectations realistic about him. He's not going to bounce back overnight. It might take years."

His face fell, but he nodded. "Fair enough. Don't hold it against me if I badger you to continue when September comes around, though. Can you start Monday?"

"I can."

"Good. Stop by tomorrow, and we'll go over everything."

Nervous excitement swirled in her stomach. Or maybe it was the greasy fish. Either way, she hoped she'd made the right decision. Chicago was behind her. She couldn't help the boys she'd left behind. But she could help Wyatt.

She just prayed she really was what Wyatt needed. She'd never forgive herself if she let him down, too.

Chapter Four

❧

Drew knocked on the fire station door Monday morning at 6:30 a.m. Boxes containing two dozen doughnuts teetered, but he tightened his hold on them. Every station he'd worked at welcomed food, especially the sweet stuff. He had a feeling he'd need every ounce of help to fit in with his new coworkers. What was the Bible passage about prophets not being accepted in their hometowns? Not a great analogy, considering he wasn't a prophet. His soul was too tarnished to even contemplate that thought.

"Gannon. You're late," Chief Reynolds barked as he let Drew in. He was in his midfifties with receding salt-and-pepper hair and a powerful upper body. He reminded Drew of a bulldog, except bulldogs were friendlier. "Follow me."

"Yes, sir." Drew kept his head high and his feet moving through the corridor. He was thirty minutes early since his shift started at seven, but hey, he understood this was Rookie Mind Games 101. He'd been through it at both his previous fire stations. Each station had its own unique way of welcoming new hires, and by welcome, he meant harass, intimidate, make fun of and generally try to wean out the ones who could handle the job from the ones who couldn't.

He could handle the job.

His coworkers just didn't know it yet.

"Listen up." The chief stopped in the kitchen, where two men and one woman stood near the coffeemaker. "This is Drew Gannon." He sent Drew a sideways glance without a hint of pleasure and nodded to the man in front of the stove. "Ben Santos. Gary Walters. Amanda Delassio." He addressed the three. "Don't bother remembering this one's name. He won't be around long enough for it to matter."

Drew shook their hands, making mental notes to keep their names straight since he didn't recognize them.

"Are you done lollygagging?" The chief marched ahead and disappeared through the first door on the left. Drew followed. "Check in at station dispatch. Sign-in's over there. We keep a daily log. Think you can handle that?"

"Yes, sir." Drew scratched his name on the list, but the chief was already out the door.

"Secretary is on duty eight until four Monday through Friday. Locker rooms are to your right. Classroom is up ahead. You'll get a key code for the supply room. We don't use radios. Every room is wired into the speaker system. I expect you to keep your ears open at all times."

Drew practically raced to keep up with him. The chief continued upstairs, filling him in on the workout room, living area and basic rules. They completed a brief tour of the garage, trucks and the equipment.

"Got all that, hotshot?"

"Yes, sir."

"You're getting off easy with a six-month probation period and only because I'm trusting the letters of recommendation from your previous supervisors. Personally, I don't see you lasting two weeks, let alone six months." The chief circled back to his office with Drew at his heels. "Be ready at seven for assignments. And let's make one thing clear—I've got no use for quitters, whiners or superstars. You're the bottom of the barrel in my station, and don't forget it."

If Drew had already been working there for a couple of years, he would have said something like, "I love you, too, Chief," and winked at the man, but he'd learned the hard way to keep his mouth shut, ears open and attitude humble until they accepted him.

If they accepted him...

They would. Eventually.

"Well, if it isn't the NFL wannabe." Tony Ludlow, a former classmate of Drew's, blocked the hallway. His beefy arms were crossed over an equally muscular chest. Drew's stomach dropped to his toes. Of all his possible coworkers, how had he ended up with Tony? They'd graduated from the same class and enjoyed a healthy competition on the football team and off, particularly with girls. Drew cringed, remembering how he'd tried to steal Tony's prom date. It was probably too late to wish he hadn't succeeded. What was that girl's name, anyhow?

"Tony." Drew stuck his hand out, but Tony didn't shake it. Surely almost fifteen years had been long enough to douse Tony's anger about the whole prom thing.

"Aren't we fortunate? The pretty boy is back," Tony said to the group in the kitchen. "I wouldn't trust him near a corpse, let alone your wives or girlfriends."

Apparently fifteen years hadn't dampened Tony's fury. *Great.*

"What about my husband?" Amanda said, smirking. "Should I be worried about this guy hitting on Jack?"

Good one, Amanda. Drew had a feeling she'd be fun to work with…someday.

"I would be, Mandy." Tony sized Drew up. "You might as well quit now. No one's going to hold your hand here."

"I'm giving him three weeks," Ben said.

Hey, it was a step up. The chief had given him only two weeks, so he must have impressed Ben more than he'd thought. A call came over the speakers, and everyone got to work.

The next several hours were spent checking equipment, learning procedures, cleaning toilets, prepping gear and responding to emergencies—two 911 calls and one fire call, which turned out to be a false alarm.

After dinner he finally had a break and managed to call Wyatt. He'd tried not to worry, but he couldn't help wondering if Lauren and Wyatt were doing okay.

"Hey, buddy, how was your day?"

"Oh, hey, Uncle Drew. It was fine." It sounded like music played in the background, but that might have been the television.

"How's it going with Lauren?"

"Okay."

The kid was a real conversationalist. Drew tried not to sigh. "Have a lot of homework?"

"No."

"What did you have for dinner?"

"Um…" Wyatt must have pulled the phone away because Drew heard Lauren's muffled voice say something. "Some noodles. Lingreeny."

"Linguine?"

"Yeah, that's it."

Drew asked a few more questions and got monosyllabic answers. "Don't watch too much TV."

"I can't. She won't let me. We're listening to music. Lauren likes *weird* stuff."

"What's weird about it?"

"I don't know. She called it jazz."

He chuckled. "Jazz, huh?"

"Yeah. If I could figure out her phone's pass code, I'd change it to something good."

"Keep your hands off her phone."

"Uncle Drew," he whined.

"I mean it. Jazz is...educational." He grimaced, thinking of the torture the poor kid was experiencing.

"Whatever."

"I love you, Wyatt."

"You, too, Uncle Drew."

They hung up.

"Hey, Gannon," Tony yelled as he entered the living room. "Locker-room floor needs mopping."

"Yes, sir," Drew said softly.

He was living the dream, all right. As much as he loved his job, he found himself eager for the shift to end. He'd forgotten how miserable the early probation period could be, and it was that much worse with Tony poisoning the rest of the crew's impressions of him.

It would be nice if they could see the man he'd become instead of the boy he used to be, but time would take care of that. If not, he'd have to majorly suck up and apologize to Tony.

Who else in town needed an apology from him?

He groaned, heading to the closet for the cleaning supplies. Maybe if he scrubbed the floor hard enough, he could erase all the damage he'd done in his teen years.

At least he didn't have to worry about Wyatt on top of everything else. The kid was in good hands. And if Lauren could see past his mistakes, the rest of the crew could, too. He hoped so, at least. He'd have to be patient and work at it.

Were frozen waffles a proper breakfast for a ten-year-old boy? Lauren plucked two out of the toaster and dropped them onto a plate. Opening the refrigerator, she scanned the shelves for fruit. A carton of orange juice stood next to a gallon of milk. Strawberries hid behind a brick of cheese. They would have to do.

She was out of her element here. Last night had been awkward. Since Wyatt had said he didn't have any homework, he'd fired up his video games as soon as he'd gotten home from school. Then, when she turned them off after an hour, he'd wanted to watch television shows she found entirely inappropriate. Dinner had been quiet. She'd turned on soothing music, but it hadn't helped.

Drew would be home in thirty minutes. Should she tell him she was having second thoughts about their arrangement?

She rinsed and sliced a few strawberries, fanning them out across the waffles. She set the plate in front of Wyatt.

"Here you go." After wiping her hands on a paper towel, she checked her watch. "What time did you say the bus picks you up?"

"Why are these things—" he grimaced, holding a strawberry slice in the air "—on my waffles?"

She propped up a smile. "They're strawberries. Full of vitamin C."

His shoulders drooped as he pushed all the strawberries to the side. His hair was sticking up in the back, but at least he'd changed into his school clothes.

"They're good. You should try them." This morning wasn't going much better than last night. She'd spent her life helping kids, but she had no experience taking care of them. "At least eat the waffles. You need some food in your stomach. It will help you learn."

Wyatt wolfed down the waffles, ignoring the berries. Lauren heard the telltale screech of brakes in the distance.

"Grab your backpack. The bus is almost here."

He trudged to the hall and slung his backpack over his shoulder. "Will you be here when I get home?"

"No, I won't. Your uncle will." She opened the front door. "Have a good day."

His eyebrows rose in worry, but he nodded and walked to the end of the drive right as the bus pulled up. Lauren waited in the doorway until he was safely on, and then she shut the door and tidied up the kitchen and living room. She was getting ready to take her first sip of coffee when Drew walked in.

"How did it go?" he asked, his eyes roaming over the room. He draped his jacket on the back of a chair and set a stack of papers on the table.

Lauren debated how to answer. The weariness in Drew's posture and the bags under his eyes set her in motion. She poured him a cup of coffee. "Do you want cream and sugar?"

He wiped both hands down his face. "No, thanks. I like it black."

She returned and set the mug on the coffee table in front of Drew before taking a seat on the couch. "Sit."

He lifted a brow, smiled and kicked back in the recliner. "Yes, sir."

"Sir?"

"Sorry." He chuckled. "Habit. I've repeated those words more times in the past twenty-four hours than I care to admit. It's going to take a long time and a lot of effort to get them to accept me."

"What do you mean?" Lauren hadn't considered he wouldn't be instantly accepted at the fire station.

He took a drink, shaking his head. "It doesn't matter. The new guy always needs to prove himself. Unfortunately, I have more to prove, given my past."

She sipped her coffee. "Is there bad blood or something?"

"Tony Ludlow is one of the crew."

"I always liked Tony," she said. He'd treated her with respect in high school. Never teased her. He'd pitched in to help with homecoming floats and fund-raisers for Students Against Teen Drinking on many occasions.

Drew's expression darkened. "Figures."

He sounded jealous. She bit back a smile.

"How was your first night with Wyatt?"

First night...and possibly only night? How honest should she be?

"Well, I slept good. Thanks for setting the room up for me." She'd been surprised to find a pullout sofa made up with a pretty butter-yellow comforter in the office.

"Of course. Do you need anything? Say the word, and we'll get it for you."

"It's perfect."

He nodded. "And Wyatt? How did it go?"

"Um, I don't know."

Drew sat up straight. "What happened? Is he okay? Did he get on the bus? Was he worried?"

"Whoa, there, tiger." She held both palms out. "Wyatt

is fine. It's me. How can I put this? Um… I don't have much experience taking care of kids."

He collapsed back into the recliner. "Is that all? No problem. You'll get the hang of it in no time. Wyatt's pretty easy. It's not like you have to change diapers or anything."

"True." She avoided eye contact. "But I don't really know what to do with him."

Drew slapped his thigh. "Easy. Homework. Video games. TV. Bed."

"Well, he said he didn't have homework. I did let him play video games for an hour, but I don't think he should be playing them all night. And the television show he wanted to watch was entirely inappropriate for a boy his age."

"What show was it?"

"*Monsters Inside Me.*"

"Oh, that's a good one." Drew grinned. "Last week a man had worms in his intestines and didn't know it. It was disgusting."

She gagged a little bit. "It sounds disgusting. And traumatizing. I turned off the TV and put on music. I suggest you do the same."

"Yeah, I heard you were playing jazz last night."

"Oh, did Wyatt like it?" She took another sip.

"He called it weird and told me he would change the channel if he knew your pass code."

Lauren was taken aback. Then she laughed. Drew joined in. A comfortable feeling spread through her, sitting here in Drew's living room, drinking coffee, chatting about Wyatt.

"Thanks again, Lauren." His voice lowered, and she had to look away from the sincerity in his eyes.

"With you watching Wyatt, well…everything else isn't so bad."

She swallowed the doubts she'd been tallying. "I don't know what I'm doing, though."

"Just be here for him. Physically be here. That's what he needs."

Exactly. She'd been overthinking it. She just needed to show up and make sure he had dinner and went to bed on time. That was it.

But maybe a few of her rules wouldn't hurt him. Less video games, no scary shows and more creative time. Couldn't hurt.

"You look beat." She got up and took her mug to the kitchen. After rinsing it out, she grabbed her purse and returned to the living room.

His eyes were already closed. Should she tell him to go to bed? She stood there and watched him a minute. Dark lashes splayed across high cheekbones. His hair was tousled. He looked vulnerable. So handsome.

She pushed the recliner's button for the footrest to extend and covered him with a soft gray throw that had been slung over the couch.

It had been a long time since she'd felt maternal. Strange, Drew brought out her nurturing side. She'd thought it had died back in Chicago.

Maybe it would have been better for them all if it had.

Nonsense. If last night proved anything, she didn't have to worry about growing too attached to Wyatt. Or Drew. She was the babysitter. That was all.

"What do you mean he's behind in school?" Drew held his phone to his ear and listened to Wyatt's teacher explain the benchmark results. "Those are just tests. They don't mean anything."

"Tests tend to reflect basic skill levels, and he hasn't been turning in his homework. I'm not trying to get Wyatt into trouble, but I wanted you to be aware of the situation."

Wyatt wasn't turning in his homework? Drew sighed. It was much easier being the fun uncle than the responsible father. "Thank you. I'll take care of it."

The past two weeks had been hectic. Work had not improved. He'd tried to apologize to Tony, but Tony wouldn't hear him out. Since then, Drew had met all the firefighters, and two had played football with him in high school, although they were younger than him. They kept bringing up old games, and he couldn't take another sentence beginning with, "Hey, remember the time you…" He wasn't sure what was worse—Tony's snide remarks or their hero worship. The chief still hated him, too.

And now this.

Wyatt wouldn't be home for almost an hour. Drew didn't know what to do or say. Should he confront him? He had a vision of himself waving papers in front of Wyatt's face, demanding to know why he wasn't doing his homework. Then it would move to ranting about how important school was, how Wyatt didn't want to have poor study habits like Drew or he'd get kicked out of college and end up working at a gas station.

Probably not the lecture Wyatt needed at this point in his life.

Lauren would know what to do. He tied his running shoes, snatched his keys off the hook and let the front door slam behind him.

Five minutes later he parked behind the hardware

store and jogged to the back entrance. Shifting his weight from one foot to the other, he pressed the intercom.

"Who is it?"

"Drew."

"Drew who?"

"Very funny." He rolled his eyes and smiled. "Do you have a minute?"

She buzzed him in. He took the steps two at a time and found himself face-to-face with a wooden door. Lauren opened it. "What's up?"

He followed her inside. Now that he was here, he was curious to see how she lived. Galley kitchen to the right. Small table and chairs in the dining area. A cream couch and matching love seat took up most of the living room. Neither would stand a chance at staying clean with him or Wyatt. They merely had to look at something that light in color for it to get dirty. She'd placed a fluffy peach rug under the coffee table, and matching pillows adorned the couches. What stood out most of all, though, were the plants. Two tall potted trees stood in opposite corners, flanking a picture window with a view of Main Street. A fern hung from the ceiling, and three other plants—one appeared to be tall grass—were placed in various spots.

"Have a seat." She waved to the couch. He admired her casual style. Jeans rolled up at the ankles and an oversize Kelly green sweatshirt. She looked natural. Fresh. "What's going on?"

He sat on the edge of the couch, knees wide, elbows resting on them. "I got a call from Wyatt's teacher, and I'm hoping you can tell me what to do."

Her hand flew to her throat. "Oh, no. What is it? He fell. He's hurt. He's missing. He's not missing, is he?"

"No, of course not. Nothing like that." The way she'd rapid-fired off the worst scenarios poked his conscience. He hadn't put any more thought into what had made her quit her job in Chicago, but from the way she reacted, he could imagine only the worst. "He's behind in school."

Her upper body seemed to dissolve as she melted into the love seat. "Oh. You had me worried."

"Well, I *am* worried. He's not turning in his assignments. And his benchmarks were low."

A huge gray tiger-striped cat appeared out of nowhere, weaving in between his legs.

"What in the world?" He hopped to his feet, glaring at the cat. "Where did that thing come from?"

Lauren rolled her eyes. "The bedroom. This is Zingo. He's the best kitty in the world, so I'd tread carefully if I were you."

He pursed his lips and, keeping his eyes glued to the cat—who continued to rub his body around Drew's leg—sat back down. The beast jumped on the couch and onto his lap. He froze. "What. Do. I. Do?"

"Well, for one, you can stop acting like a big baby. He's a cat, not a poisonous snake."

"I can see that," he snapped.

"Pet him." She widened her eyes in emphasis and pointed at the feline.

He'd never been around cats. Didn't they carry diseases? Or kill babies? He'd heard rumors…

Gingerly, he touched Zingo's back. "Hey, he's soft."

"Duh."

Zingo curled up on his lap. "Is this normal?" When she nodded, he shrugged. "Okay, then. Back to the problem. What am I going to do about Wyatt?"

Lauren crossed one leg over the other and lifted her finger to her chin. "Hmm…"

He patted the cat's head. It started purring. He decided to ignore it.

"Did the teacher say he's behind in all his subjects or certain ones?"

"Math. Doesn't know how to multiply. He does okay in reading, but his writing needs work."

Lauren bridged her fingers. "Are you going over his homework with him at night?"

"He never has any."

"Yeah, he tells me the same. Obviously, he does have homework and is choosing not to deal with it."

"And lying about it." Drew clenched his jaw. He hated lies. "Unacceptable."

"You look mad. Are you going to say something to him?"

"Of course. I can't let him get away with lying."

"Right. You're right, but…" She frowned. "Maybe I should be there, too."

"Why?"

"To keep it peaceful."

"I'm not going to coddle him about this. He needs to be responsible."

"This isn't about coddling. It's about your approach. He needs to feel it's safe to make mistakes."

Exactly why Drew had come here in the first place— to get her opinion. He sat back, mindlessly stroking the cat's fur. "All right. What do you suggest?"

"Let's go back to your place, and when he gets home, we'll talk to him. Together."

He almost closed his eyes in relief. *Together.* The best word he'd heard since taking custody of Wyatt. "I'll drive."

Forty-five minutes later, after Wyatt had gotten off the bus, they all sat around the kitchen table, munching on a plate of grapes and cheese Lauren had thrown together. Wyatt popped one grape in after another. Drew glanced at her, and she nodded.

"Your teacher called today. Seems she's missing some of your homework."

Wyatt stopped chewing and stared at the table. "She must have lost it."

"Wyatt—" His voice rose. Lauren touched his arm.

"I don't recall you bringing any home." Lauren gestured to Wyatt.

He swallowed. "I do it at school."

"All of it?" she asked.

He nodded. Drew regained his composure. "Listen, buddy, homework is important."

"Dad didn't make me do it." Scowling, Wyatt crossed his arms over his chest.

"Since when?" Drew asked. "You can't pull that one on me. We've been together for years. School's always been important."

"I don't need it. I'm going to be a football player like Dad when I grow up."

Drew wasn't touching this topic. He hadn't talked to Wyatt about Chase's no-football decree because it hadn't come up. He did *not* want to get into it now.

"Your dad had to get into college to play football," Lauren said. "He was required to get good grades."

"Really?" Wyatt tilted his head slightly.

Saved by Lauren. Again.

"He worked hard at school." Drew leaned back in his chair. "You know we were roommates. He pulled plenty of all-nighters studying for tests. Did you know he has a degree in marketing?"

"I didn't know that."

"Yep."

"If it's okay with you, Drew," Lauren said, "let's make a new rule. The first thing Wyatt does after school is homework. Drew will help you with it when he's home, and I'll help when he's at work."

"First thing?" Wyatt whined. "Can't I have a snack first?"

"Of course you can have a snack." Drew grew serious. "But, Wyatt, I don't want you lying to me. If you're going to grow up to be a man of integrity, you have to tell the truth."

Wyatt nodded. "I'm sorry, Uncle Drew."

He held his arms out, and Wyatt fell into them. Drew met Lauren's eyes and mouthed, "Thank you." She'd taken a potentially volatile situation and made it okay. It felt good to have someone in his corner for once.

At least one person in this town was on his side.

Chapter Five

"Snack time is over. Haul out the books." Lauren clapped her hands the next afternoon. Wyatt looked like he'd just brushed his teeth with vinegar. Drew had said Wyatt just needed her to be present, and that was what she'd been for the handful of times she'd stayed with him so far. But now she had a mission to help Wyatt improve his grades—whether he wanted help or not. "I printed out worksheets to help you with multiplication."

"Those are for babies. I already know how to multiply." Wyatt pressed the tips of his fingers against the cracker crumbs and licked them. "We learned it last year."

"Good. Then you'll get through these really quick."

He let out the most pitiful sigh she'd ever heard. How did one motivate a ten-year-old boy to want to learn? Math was important. School was important.

"C'mon," she said. "The sooner you get these done, the sooner we can get out of here."

His eyes lit up, almost gold in color. "Where are we going?"

"I'm taking you to my parents' house." She gestured

to his backpack, and he grunted but took folders and books out of it. "Mom and Dad are cooking us lasagna."

"I thought your dad died."

"My birth father died. My birth mother, too. I'm taking you to meet my parents, the ones who raised me. They adopted me when I was seven. I think you'll like them. They live on the other side of the lake."

Wyatt clicked through a short piece of lead in his mechanical pencil until a new one worked its way down. As he opened a blue folder, Lauren took the seat next to him at the table.

"How did your mom die?" His freckles emphasized his innocent face. She wanted to kiss his forehead, which was ridiculous. He wasn't her son. But this was the first time he'd asked anything of her beyond, "Why can't I play another hour of 'Minecraft'?" and "Please, can I have another brownie?" The urge to share her past with him pressed on her heart.

She didn't want to burden him. Would talking about her messed-up past confuse him more?

She remembered when a girl in her third-grade class announced to everyone her parents had adopted a new brother for her. Part of Lauren had rejoiced the girl was so excited to have an adopted sibling, but the other part wanted to blend in with her classmates and hide the fact that she was adopted. Since the Pierces had moved to Lake Endwell when Lauren was in second grade, it wasn't common knowledge she wasn't their natural-born child. That day had made her feel less alone, knowing other kids got adopted, too. In fact, the other girl's attitude had changed her view of herself, paving the way for her to accept the fact that her parents wanted her the same way her classmate wanted her new brother.

Telling Wyatt about her past might help him feel less alone, too.

With her elbow on the table, Lauren rested her cheek against her palm. "My mother died when I was two. She was a drug addict, and she died of an overdose."

"Really?" Wyatt turned to face her, his feet dangling and kicking as if they couldn't take being immobile on the floor. "My mom did drugs. But she didn't die from them. She quit. It was Len who killed her."

"Yeah, well, in a way drugs did kill your mom."

"No, they didn't." His voice rose. "She went to rehab."

"I know." She gave him a tender smile. "I guess I meant when you get mixed up in drugs, you put yourself in a dangerous situation. If she wouldn't have hung around people who liked that lifestyle, she wouldn't have met Len."

"I wish she'd never met him. It's all his fault. I'm glad Dad tried to kill him. I wish he would have!" Two red spots blared from his cheeks. The outburst seemed to deflate him, though, and he laid his forehead against his arm on the table.

Her throat knotted. She lightly touched Wyatt's hunched back, and when his slender frame shook with silent tears, she scooted closer, rubbing small circles between his shoulders. "I know. I know."

She put her arm around him and pressed her cheek to his hair. He sat up with wet eyes and wiped the back of his sleeve across his face.

"You probably think I'm a big baby for crying." His face couldn't look more miserable.

"Why would I think that?"

"Men aren't supposed to cry."

"Says who? Jesus cried. When we're sad, we cry. It's

healthy. Relieves the tension building up inside. If you don't cry, the tension comes out in a bad way."

"Like how?" He sniffed again.

"Well." She looked at the ceiling briefly. "Some people get mad and yell at whoever is there for no reason. That's not good. Or what about this? Sometimes when I'm sad, I don't want to cry or feel bad, so I eat a bunch of cookies. Then I feel even worse!"

"I'd rather eat cookies than cry."

She laughed. "I would, too. But even if you eat half a bag of cookies, the sadness is still there. You just have a stomachache, too."

"Don't tell Uncle Drew I cried." His eyebrows dipped in a pleading manner.

She pretended to zip her lips and throw away the key.

"Why'd you do that?"

"It's like zipping your lips and locking it."

"That's weird."

"Yeah, well, that's how we kept promises back in my day."

Wyatt pulled out a homework paper and stared at it a minute. Then he turned to her. "Did Jesus really cry?"

Lauren nodded, swiping her phone. She opened her favorite Bible app and typed in 'Lazarus.' When the passage came up, she showed it to him. "Right here. *John* 11:35, 'Jesus wept.'"

"Why?"

She filled him in on how Jesus's friend Lazarus had died, and Jesus went to comfort the man's sisters, Mary and Martha. "Then Jesus raised Lazarus from the dead."

"That's pretty cool." Wyatt flicked his pencil against the edge of the table.

"Listen, Wyatt." She needed to proceed with caution here. What she wanted to say was important, but Wyatt might not take it very well. "I totally get why you hate Len and wish he was dead. But the anger inside you doesn't hurt Len. It only hurts you."

"I hate him," he said through gritted teeth. "I'll always hate him."

"When you're ready, when hating him feels too heavy, pray for him. That's all. Give your anger to God."

"I'm not praying for him. Ever."

She held her hands up near her chest. "Okay. That's your choice. Forgiveness has a way of giving a person peace, though."

"He killed my mom." It sounded less adamant than his previous declaration.

"Yep, he did, and he's being punished for it."

"Forgiving him is like saying what he did doesn't matter, like it was okay for him to kill her. It's not okay."

Oh, how well she understood his thinking. Life would be so much easier if the people she'd needed to forgive had acknowledged they'd hurt her. The thought of forgiving them had felt like it would be giving them a free pass to treat her terribly.

"Forgiveness is a tricky thing. It's not about acting as if the person didn't hurt you. It's about moving on with your life and letting God be their judge. Some of the people you'll forgive won't even feel sorry for the things they've done to you."

"That's why I'm not forgiving. They have to at least say they're sorry."

"Forgiving someone who never apologizes is one of the most difficult things you'll ever do."

Wyatt blew out a breath. "I don't think I can."

"I understand. It's hard. But it's also the best thing you can do for yourself. Forgiving someone doesn't erase the hurt, but it helps you move forward." Lauren drew him into a half embrace. He didn't pull away.

"Do I have to right now?"

She chuckled. "No, silly. When you're ready, pray for God to help you with it."

"What if I'm never ready?"

She'd thought the same thing many times. She'd forgiven a lot in her life, given her anger and pain to God the way she'd just advised Wyatt to, but… She frowned. She hadn't gotten around to forgiving the people responsible for destroying Treyvon's and Jay's lives. How did one forgive nameless faces?

What about me? How can I sit here and preach to this kid when I haven't spent two minutes in prayer about those boys other than to blame God for letting it happen?

"You will be ready." *And I will be, too.* She patted his back. "Now, let's get this homework figured out."

A few hours later, Wyatt had finished his spelling homework, written a sloppy paragraph about insects and failed more than half the multiplication problems on the worksheet before they called it quits and drove to her folks' house. Lauren sighed. She didn't know how parents did it. How did they keep up with the emotional ups and downs, as well as schoolwork, activities and making sure the kids were fed, dressed and healthy? It was exhausting.

She sat with her mom on the deck overlooking the backyard. Wyatt and Lauren's dad were attempting to fly a kite on the spacious lawn. So far it hadn't flown more than four feet in the air, and they were currently untangling the line. Again.

"What time is it?" she asked her mom. Mom had

turned sixty a month ago, but she didn't look her age. Tonya Pierce had short brown hair and the kindest eyes Lauren had ever seen. She described herself as "fluffy," but her cute turquoise capris and T-shirt hid her extra pounds.

"Almost seven, why?"

"I need to have Wyatt back to his house by eight. His dad, Chase, is calling him." Lauren had to hand it to Chase; he called Wyatt two or three times a week. Drew kept a log of each phone call, too, for Chase's lawyer. The log would help Chase reestablish his parental rights when he was released. Lauren wasn't sure how she felt about that. The guy hadn't put Wyatt's needs first when he went on his revenge spree. Would he be the dad Wyatt needed when he was released?

"What do you think of him?" Mom crossed one ankle over the other.

"Chase? I don't know. I haven't met him. He's good about calling Wyatt." She hoped Chase was worthy of being Wyatt's father. The boy had been through too much. He needed someone he could count on. A rock who wouldn't budge.

Drew came to mind. For a rock, he was surprisingly flexible about many things. She'd been impressed he actually came to her for advice about the homework situation.

"Did you hear back from the woman in Chicago?"

"I talked to her this morning." Lauren swirled the straw in her glass of iced tea. "I spent a few hours researching everything she told me, and honestly, Mom, I'm not sure if I should bother looking into it more. I don't think it's going to work out."

"Why not?"

"I would need a large building, permits, insurance

and equipment. Add the uniforms, tournament fees and teachers' salaries, and I don't think it makes financial sense."

"But she's successful at running one, right?"

"Yes, but hers is in a suburb of Chicago. Lake Endwell isn't big, and it's a thirty-minute drive to Kalamazoo. I doubt I'd get enough students to make it worthwhile."

Mom made a clucking sound with her tongue. "I see what you're saying."

Her dad let out a whoop as Wyatt jogged by holding the string, making the bird-shaped kite soar higher. She snapped a photo of him and texted it to Drew.

"Nice job, Wyatt," Lauren yelled. He gave her a thumbs-up.

"He's a cute kid."

"He is."

"I'm glad you're taking care of him."

"Yeah, well, it's just for the summer. I need to figure out my long-term plans."

"Oh, that reminds me. I found out some interesting news. The varsity cheer coach, Joanna Mills, is quitting."

Lauren sipped her drink. "So?"

"So, you'd be perfect for the job."

"I don't think they pay much to cheerleading coaches." Lauren pulled her hair to the side.

"I've got Joanna's number. Give her a call. Find out what's involved. It couldn't hurt."

It probably couldn't. The cheer academy looked like a no go, and Lauren trusted her mom. She gave great advice and usually didn't stick her nose into Lauren's personal affairs.

"Give me the number. I'll call." Maybe this fit the old saying about one door closing and another opening. She doubted a cheerleading coach earned enough to support herself, but she could combine it with another part-time job if needed.

What about my future? Retirement? Fulfillment?

"You seem a little better lately, honey." Mom had a knack for seeing right into her soul.

"I feel a little better."

"Taking care of Wyatt is good for you."

"For now. Hopefully I'm helping him."

"You are. Look at him." She hitched her chin toward the lawn. The kite had fallen, and Wyatt and Dad were winding the string again. "Resilient, considering all he's been through. But you would know, too, wouldn't you? You went through a lot of the same things."

"Not everything. His dad loves him and wants a relationship with him."

"You're not jealous, are you?"

Lauren laughed. "Of course not! Why would you think such a thing? I'm happy for him."

"Good."

They stared out at the pretty green lawn. The woods' edge cast shadows in the distance, but the evening sunshine warmed Lauren's arms.

"Haven't seen you in church in a while."

Lauren's good mood darkened. "No, you haven't."

"Why don't you join us Sunday? We'll pick you up."

"I'll think about it."

Mom raised her eyebrows. "You've been saying that for five months."

"And you've been saying *that* for five months."

"I care, Lauren. I care about you. I care about your soul. Don't shut God out."

Lauren sat up, rubbing her arms. "I'm not."

"Then come with us."

"Mom, I need to do this on my own terms. I'm not going to be guilted into going back to church. I don't think God wants that. Doesn't He want a cheerful giver?"

"Oh, Lauren…"

Thankfully, Mom dropped the topic. How could Lauren explain something she didn't understand herself? Of all the cases she'd worked on, all the kids born into negligent, dangerous homes, Treyvon and Jay had affected her the most. And right when she'd been close to helping them, tragedy had struck. God could have stepped in, but He didn't. And she still loved God, but she couldn't quite trust Him.

Trust and love. Faith and hope.

All intertwined.

Without one, could she have the others?

And how could she keep talking to Wyatt about faith and forgiveness and God's love when she'd been shutting God out for months? No matter how many sips of tea she took, Lauren was left with the taste of ashes.

Shaking the raindrops off his jacket, Drew hung his keys on the hook and nudged the front door shut behind him. Yawning, he tried to erase last night's scene. The car wreck had been fatal. Gruesome. He went straight to the bathroom to wash his hands before hunting for Lauren. First stop, the kitchen.

"You didn't have to make breakfast, Lauren." He paused in the doorway at the welcome sight. A stack of French toast steamed from a plate, the coffeemaker gurgled and bacon sizzled from the frying pan.

"I know." She smiled sweetly, spatula in hand. "But I made Wyatt French toast, so I figured you might want some, too."

"I do." Was his exhaustion playing tricks on him, or was she even more beautiful than before? Her hair flowed behind her, sending his previously comatose pulse into high gear. The house smelled delicious, all sugar and spice and everything nice.

Rain streamed down the windows. Lauren switched the light on over the table and set a platter loaded with bacon in the center. Drew poured two mugs of coffee as she took a seat.

"Mind if I say grace?" he asked. She bowed her head and folded her hands. He said the prayer, then sliced into his stack of French toast. He savored the light texture and maple syrup. "Mmm...delicious."

"Glad you like them." She beamed. "Did you put out any fires?"

"No, but Tony and I were sent on a nasty call last night." A shudder rippled down his spine. The only good thing about the night? It had opened a crack in Tony's granite-hard attitude about him. Tony had actually told him he'd done nice work out there. It was a start.

"That bad, huh?" Worry lines creased between her eyes.

"Yeah, it was." Outside the station, he never discussed the fires, 911 calls or accidents he responded to, but that might be because he had no one to discuss them with. A glance at Lauren had him biting his tongue. He wouldn't ruin her day with tales of twisted limbs and death.

"Was it the accident out on Ridge Road?" She took a drink of coffee, staring at him over the rim of her cup.

"Yeah, how did you know?"

"I get local news updates on Facebook. I was hoping you weren't called to that one. It looked horrible."

"It was." He set his fork down for a moment, trying

to push away the visions in his head, but they kept coming, making his blood pressure climb.

"Tell me about it."

"I don't think so. You don't want to hear it."

"I can handle it."

Could she? He doubted it. She obviously couldn't handle all the bad things she'd witnessed in Chicago or she wouldn't have quit to hide away here.

That must be his exhaustion talking. He didn't think less of her for moving.

"It might help to talk about it." Her gray eyes probed, saw too much.

"You first." He bit into a piece of bacon, too tired to think straight. "What happened in Chicago?"

She suddenly grew very absorbed in the half-eaten food on her plate. With her fork, she pushed a bite deeper into the syrup pooling around her French toast. Seconds ticked by with only the sound of the rain coming down.

"See?" he said. "Talking about it doesn't help."

Her fork dropped with a clatter. "You're wrong. I...I just wish..."

"What?" He lowered his tone, smoothing out the edge to it. "What do you wish?"

She pushed her chair back and turned away from him to look out the window. *Nice going, Gannon.* The woman had made him bacon—bacon!—so why was he picking on her? She was doing *him* the favor by taking care of Wyatt, and here he was, asking questions he knew she didn't want to discuss.

He admired the graceful line of her neck as she continued to stare at the rivulets of water streaming down the glass. When the silence had stretched too long, he opened his mouth to apologize, but she started to speak.

"I worked for child welfare services in some of the rougher neighborhoods of Chicago, and I was used to hard cases. I mean, eight years of being surrounded by poverty coats you with Teflon. Sometimes I'd go home and wonder if I was getting burned-out. But then I'd remember why I got into the field, and I would keep going."

He wanted to ask why she got into the field, but she continued. "Treyvon and Jay were brothers. Treyvon was fifteen. Jay was twelve. They lived in Englewood. I always dreaded cases from that part of town."

When she didn't say anything, he cleared his throat. "What's wrong with Englewood?"

She jerked, meeting his eyes. "Poverty. Gangs. Drugs. Way back when I first moved to Chicago, I was assigned a case that brought me in contact with an elderly Englewood resident. From that point on, Mr. Bell watched out for me whenever I had to make home visits, which wasn't very often. Regardless, I never went alone, always had a coworker go with me."

Drew stopped chewing as her words sunk in. *Home visits. Rough areas.* She'd willingly put herself in dangerous situations. His chest felt tight. He hated that she'd been around criminals.

"In Jay's situation, a teacher filed a report, and I was assigned his case. He'd been a model student, and one of the few kids in the class who showed up regularly. The teacher noticed he was absent more often and was distracted at school. She called his mother and realized his home situation had deteriorated. I conducted the routine interviews. He was a nice kid. Smart and polite. Treyvon was, too."

Drew reached for his coffee, frowning as he processed more of the words. Like her use of the word *was*.

"Didn't take long to find out his grandmother had been living with them and their drug-addicted mom. A few months prior to the teacher filing the report, the grandma had a stroke and was moved to a nursing home to recover. Jay's life—and Treyvon's—had dissolved into chaos. I'll spare you the details of their situation, but neither had the clothing, food or supervision necessary. I was doing my best to work with their mother to create a healthy home situation until the grandmother could return home."

"Wait." He raised his hand. "They still lived with their mom even though she was on drugs? For how long?"

"I'd been working with them for about a month. I convinced her to get a family friend to live with them until the grandmother was released. The doctor's reports were promising. Although her speech was slurred, her right side had regained enough mobility for her to walk with a walker. Their grandma was expected to be home within a few weeks."

"But why let those boys stay there at all?" He couldn't wrap his head around it.

"We work with the children's family to fix problems first as long as the kids aren't in danger. Their mom agreed to ask her friend to stay, and that alone solved several of the issues. She also agreed to a treatment program."

"I see." He didn't, though. Not really. Kids shouldn't live around drugs.

"It's next to impossible to place two adolescent boys into a foster home. Treyvon flat out told me he'd run away with Jay if they couldn't stay together. They'd been well taken care of by their grandmother. My hope was when she returned, they would go back to their normal life."

He took a drink of lukewarm coffee, dreading the way the story was heading.

"Long story short, the grandmother got pneumonia and died unexpectedly. The family friend moved out. I had two weeks to place both kids in foster homes. I tried so hard to keep them together. I called everyone on my list."

"You couldn't help it if they had to be separated."

Her eyes, silver with unshed tears, met his. "They didn't have time to be separated. Jay was shot in a drive-by. Gunned down on a sidewalk. Twelve. A boy his age shouldn't be outside at one in the morning, and especially not in that neighborhood. I know he was looking for Treyvon."

Drew pushed his plate back, no longer hungry. "Where was Treyvon?"

"Robbing a mini-mart. One of the local gangs recruited him. That's exactly what I worried about when he told me he would run away. The odds of escaping gang life when you have nowhere to go and aren't old enough to have a job aren't good."

Drew sucked in a breath. He felt bad about the kids, but Lauren worked in gang areas? How much danger had she been in all those years? Unwanted scenarios, all bad, popped up in his head, but he shook them away.

"So Jay—did he make it?" He reached over, covering her hand on the table with his. She didn't pull it away, which he took as a good sign.

"He died near a vacant lot two blocks from his house." Her flat tone worried him. "And Treyvon's in a juvenile detention center until he's of age."

"I'm sorry, Lauren." He stood and pulled her into his arms, inhaling the coconut smell of her shampoo as her head leaned against his shoulder. She wrapped her arms around his waist. Having her in his arms felt right even if it was only to comfort her.

She took a slight step back, but he kept his arms around her.

"I should have gotten them out of there sooner. I failed them, Drew. They were good kids. They tried hard to rise above their situation, and I was their liaison. I was supposed to help them, and both their lives are ruined because of me."

Tipping her chin up with his finger, he looked her in the eyes. "Hey, it's not your fault. How were you supposed to know their grandmother would die? Or Treyvon would join a gang?"

"I knew the signs. Kids in that neighborhood were always being pressured to join one of the local gangs. All the gang members had to do was threaten to hurt one of their loved ones…" She shivered. "Jay and Treyvon were acting secretive when I met with them those final two weeks. I told myself they were sad about their grandmother. That they were worried about what would happen to them. I should have put two and two together."

"Don't do this to yourself, Lauren."

She slipped out of his grasp, rubbing her biceps, and faced the window. "It's hard. I saw so much potential in Jay. When I think of him shot down—he was just a boy. I made him promises I didn't keep."

"Didn't or couldn't? There's a difference, you know." Drew put his hand on her shoulder. She glanced up at him, her expression pleading for something—redemption maybe—but she turned, picked up her mug and padded to the kitchen. He followed her. She shut the microwave door and jabbed the buttons until the machine whirred to life.

"What does it matter now? He's dead. Another bright

light in this world snuffed out. I thought I could make a difference…" She leaned against the counter.

"You did make a difference."

"Now who's lying?" She let out a brittle laugh and ran her fingers through her hair. "Never mind. I should get going."

"Your coffee hasn't finished warming up."

"I'm not thirsty anymore."

She grabbed her purse, but Drew held on to her arm. He should let her leave, but everything inside him screamed to make her stay. "Wait. Don't you want to hear about the accident last night?"

She shook her head. "You were right. I can't handle it." And she left.

Drew stared at the closed door. She'd handled far worse than he did. He was a first responder, detached from the personal lives of the victims he helped. He didn't blame her for quitting, but why had she stayed with it for all those years to begin with?

Was it selfish to be relieved she was no longer a social worker? Too dangerous. When he thought of her walking through gang areas, making visits to drug addicts' homes…he wanted to lock her up and keep her from ever being in danger again. She was sunshine, a bright light to protect and cherish.

But she wasn't his.

At least she wasn't in Chicago anymore. He liked her right here in sleepy Lake Endwell.

He just hoped he hadn't pushed her too far.

Lauren's windshield wipers swiped angrily as she drove away from Drew's. Gripping the steering wheel, her hands trembled.

Don't think. Just go.

When life got to be too much, she would drive to a secluded area several miles out of town. On warm days, she'd stroll along the path next to the river. On rainy days like today, she'd sit in her car and soak in the view of the trees and river for as long as possible. The place soothed her in a way she couldn't explain. She'd missed this spot when she lived in Chicago.

As soon as she drove into the deserted parking lot, her tension lowered a bit. She flexed her hands open and shut a few times and forced her jaw to relax. Even through the rain, the bright green leaves on the trees looked supple and new.

Drew was right. She should have found Treyvon and Jay foster homes from the start.

But their situation had been so tricky. She'd been sure their grandmother would come home. Treyvon had been adamant about not getting separated from Jay. And their mother had agreed to drug counseling. Lauren had convinced her to get another responsible adult in the household. The woman had complied.

How had it gone so wrong?

Why, Lord? Why did it have to happen that way? Why did You let it happen?

The ping of rain against the roof was the only answer.

Her chest felt as if it were being squeezed by a giant clamp. She choked back threatening tears, refusing to give in to the hopelessness that wouldn't subside.

Her phone dinged. She glanced at it. Drew texted, Are you okay?

No, she was not okay. She might never be okay.

Jesus wept. She could hear her voice saying those words to Wyatt.

She was the world's biggest hypocrite. Always had an answer for everyone else but didn't take her own advice.

Okay, God. I told Wyatt to give his anger to You. But I haven't given mine up. I'm clinging to it, and I don't know why.

Because like Wyatt had said, forgiveness seemed like a free pass. Like what happened didn't matter.

Lord, help me release my anger. I want to stop being angry with You. With me. Even with Treyvon. I don't know how. I can't make any sense of why Jay died. Why? Why did it have to end so badly?

An old Bible verse came to mind, something about God working all things out for the good of those who loved Him.

She typed in her Bible app. But before the results showed up, she closed her eyes. Could she really believe God worked *all* things out for good? Even the horrible, sinful, evil things?

She didn't want bad things worked out for good. She wanted them good to begin with. Shouldn't Wyatt be living with his father? Shouldn't Jay and Treyvon's grandmother have lived? Shouldn't both boys still be going to school?

She closed the app and tossed her phone in her purse.

The anger she'd work on, but she wasn't ready to forgive. Not God, not the shooters, not the gang members, not Treyvon. Not even herself.

She might never be ready.

Chapter Six

Two weeks later, Lauren tapped her foot and checked the clock above Joanna Mills's desk in the art room at the elementary school. She had exactly fourteen minutes before Wyatt got out of school. Once she signed him out, they planned on surprising Drew with treats at the fire station for his one-month anniversary. After she told Drew everything about Chicago, they had fallen back into their routine. He didn't ask probing questions, and she kept her focus on Wyatt, where it belonged. And now two dozen chocolate cupcakes fresh from the Daily Donut were nestled in her backseat, but Joanna still hadn't returned to the art room.

"Sorry about that. I found it." Joanna licked her finger and rifled through a folder before selecting a paper. "Here it is. Everything you need to know about getting certified to be a cheerleading coach. The program goes over a lot of stuff like keeping the cheerleaders healthy and preventing injuries. It's worth the time."

Lauren scanned the paper. "Thank you."

"No problem." Joanna smiled, setting the folder on top of a teetering stack of papers. "Did you know they need another high school counselor? Great hours. Typical pay. You really should apply for the position. You'll have a much better chance at getting hired as the coach if you're employed by the school."

School counselor? Lauren didn't realize a position was open. The very words sent dread from her head to her toes. "I'm not interested."

"No? I thought you used to be a social worker. Seems like a great fit. But, then, it's pretty tame around here. I don't blame you if sending transcripts to colleges and changing kids' schedules isn't your dream job."

Sending transcripts and fixing schedules actually sounded quite nice.

"Tell me more about the position."

Joanna filled her in on what she knew. Lauren had to admit it appealed to her, but she didn't have time to think about it. She needed to sign Wyatt out. He would worry if she wasn't waiting for him. "Thank you. I'll think about it, but I have to run."

Joanna followed her to the door. "Go online and fill out the application. There will be about a million hoops to jump through, but don't let that stop you."

"Thanks, Joanna. I appreciate it."

Twenty minutes later, Lauren and Wyatt rolled down the car windows on the way to the fire station.

"Can you believe it's June already?" Lauren grinned. "How many days left of school?"

"Four." Wyatt tipped his head back as the wind blasted his face. "I can't wait! Jackson and Levi told me they're playing football this summer. It starts in August. I have a sign-up form. It's going to be awesome!"

Lauren frowned. *Football.* Hadn't Drew told her Wyatt wasn't allowed to play? She made a mental note to ask him about it later. "What about Hunter?"

Wyatt's face fell. "I don't know. I think he plays soccer. But all the cool kids are playing football. Levi's dad is coaching. I hope I get on his team."

"The cool kids, huh?" She waited for the traffic light to turn green. "Isn't Hunter a cool kid?"

Wyatt mumbled something.

"What was that? I couldn't hear you?"

"Hunter's nice, but Jackson and Levi..."

When he didn't elaborate, she prodded. "Are cool?" There was his smile. He nodded happily.

She parked the car and figured she'd talk to Drew about the football situation later. "Here. You take a box, and I'll take a box. Together we might get all twenty-four of these yum-yums into the station without dropping any."

"Yum-yums?" Wyatt shook his head, acting disgusted. But he held his hands out for her to set one of the boxes in them. "You have the weirdest sayings, Lauren."

"Weird? *Moi?* You should be glad you have me around to enlighten you." Grinning, she held the other box and shut the door with her backside. Wyatt fell in beside her. Tony Ludlow let them into the station, and they followed him to the kitchen.

"What's this?" Tony tried to lift the cover of her cupcake box.

"No peeking." She gave him a fake frown. "Is Drew around?"

His smile faltered, but he hitched his chin. "Sure. I'll get him."

Drew appeared. "Why are you guys here?" The twinkle in his eyes contained more than simple happiness. He looked genuinely surprised. Hadn't he ever been the recipient of a nice gesture before?

"It's your one-month anniversary. We thought we

should celebrate it." Lauren winked at Wyatt, who lifted the lid off the boxes. The cupcakes spelled out, "Thank You, Drew and Station 4."

"You did this for me?" Drew gazed at her intently, then pulled Wyatt into a hug. "Wow, thank you."

"Well, go on." Lauren waved at the box. "Try one."

Two guys joined them. "What's this? Oh, hey, Wyatt, how's it going?"

Wyatt fist-bumped the men, clearly familiar with them, and Lauren watched in amusement as they interacted. Like wolves catching a whiff of a fresh kill, the rest of the crew filled the kitchen. Drew introduced Lauren to the people she didn't know. Tony strolled back in and read the lettering on the cupcakes.

"Drew, huh?" Tony sniffed, grinning at her. "Be honest. You did this to thank *me*—didn't you Lauren?"

She laughed, glancing at Drew. He'd frozen with half a cupcake in his hand, the other half in his mouth.

"You think so?" Lauren punched Tony's arm lightly. "And I suppose you're the king of the station around here."

"I get the job done." His smug expression made her chuckle. "Unlike your boyfriend here."

Boyfriend? She sputtered. Tony thought she and Drew were...dating? *Absurd!*

But...the idea wasn't horrible. She darted a peek at Drew's lips. Chocolate-frosted lips.

"Who's dating Gannon?" one of the guys yelled out.

"Well, there goes my chance with her," another one muttered.

Wyatt looked excited, doubtful and a tad confused.

"Hold on there." Drew held his palms out. "We're not dating."

Lauren blinked, oddly disappointed Drew sounded

so adamant about it. They chatted with everyone, and within minutes, the cupcakes were gone. Drew walked Lauren and Wyatt to the door. "Thanks for doing this. It means a lot to me."

"You're welcome."

"Hey, can you stick around for a while when I get home tomorrow?"

"Why?" Her stomach started twirling.

The intensity in his stare didn't help her tummy. "I have something I want to talk to you about. I'll bring breakfast."

Lauren nodded and nudged Wyatt to the parking lot. Drew was bringing her breakfast. She liked the sound of that. But what did he want to talk to her about?

She guessed she'd find out in the morning.

Drew juggled the paper bag filled with carryout containers from Pat's Diner in his hand as he fumbled with his keys to unlock the front door the next morning. Ever since that idiot Tony had said the word *boyfriend* about him and Lauren, Drew had been hammered with endless comments about how hot Lauren was, and how she was a legend in high school, and why hadn't she gotten married, and maybe Miggs or Dan had a chance. At least Tony was married, so Drew hadn't had to listen to him go on and on about Lauren.

He'd wanted to smash cupcakes in the other guys' faces. But that wasn't acceptable behavior, and the cupcakes had been long gone at that point, so he'd had to grit his teeth and not say a word. Not one word. Or they would tease him mercilessly the rest of his working days.

He was still on extremely thin ice where his coworkers were concerned. Sure, he and Tony had been getting along slightly better. But the chief continued to harass him. Drew always got the worst cleanup jobs, and he wouldn't be assigned driving duty until the probation period was over. He was the backup, the *probie*, and it bugged him.

But not as much as the thought of Lauren dating one of the guys from work.

Or anyone.

Except him.

Like she would ever go out with him. Not a chance. It would be a bad idea, anyhow. If they dated and it didn't work out, she'd quit watching Wyatt. And speaking of Wyatt, Drew needed some advice. He opened the front door.

"Hey," she said. "You survived another day at work."

His mouth went dry at the sight of Lauren standing in the living room with no makeup on, her hair flowing around her shoulders. She wore a white short-sleeved button-down shirt with ankle-length fitted jeans.

"Why don't we eat outside?" Lauren slipped a pair of sandals on and strode to the patio door. "Leave the bag out there, and I'll get plates and coffee."

Drew crossed the room. After setting the bag on the table, he held his hand up to the bright sun. *June already.* Man, he loved summer. Maybe he could take Wyatt out canoeing later.

"Give me a minute to change," he called on his way to his bedroom. He shrugged into a T-shirt and khaki shorts, then joined her on the back deck. She'd already transferred the omelets and hash browns to plates and sat with a satisfied grin under the maroon umbrella.

"You look happy," he said.

"I am. Isn't it a beautiful day?"

The day wasn't the only thing that was beautiful. He

lunged for his coffee cup, scalding his tongue when he took a drink. "Yeah, it's nice out."

Soon they dug into the food on their plates. A trickling sound from the waterfall flowing into the ornamental pond punctuated the peace of the day. The yard wasn't overly large, but it was encased by a privacy fence and had mature trees around it. He liked it. Not too much to mow but big enough to host a barbecue.

"Thanks for bringing Wyatt over yesterday and for the cupcakes. Everyone loved them."

"You're welcome. He was very excited. He thinks the fire station is one of the best places on earth."

"Well, he's not alone." Drew grinned, unsure of how to broach what was on his mind. "Can I ask you something?"

"Sure."

"Chase wants me to bring Wyatt to visit him. Do you think it's a good idea?"

She finished chewing before replying. "It depends. Have you asked Wyatt what he wants?"

"Not yet. I wanted to run it by you first." He blew across the top of his mug, hoping the coffee would be cool enough to drink without becoming a burn victim.

"Do you know what's involved?"

He'd talked to Chase about it. "Yeah. For the most part."

"Does the correctional facility have a children's room or a comfortable area for Wyatt to be with Chase?"

"They have a visitor's room with a children's area. I'm already on the approved list, but we'd have to schedule the visit." He leaned back in his chair. It didn't seem too complicated. Apply for a visit, adhere to the dress code and flash some identification.

"Good. But don't rush into a decision." She twisted

her lips as if trying to decide what to say. "Prisons are pretty intimidating. The property itself might stress Wyatt out with the fences and barbed wire. Plus he'll have to go through a metal detector and be around other inmates. I don't know if it's wise at this time."

He stared out at the green lawn, where a few dandelions had poked through. His present view was the opposite of what Lauren had just described—fencing, barbed wire, metal detectors and other inmates. Did he want Wyatt to have those images in his mind?

"That being said, in my professional opinion, kids need relationships with their parents, and the courts will be more likely to reinstate Chase's parental rights if he maintains contact with Wyatt."

"Chase told me that, too. Plus he really misses the kid. Wyatt was his life."

She dusted crumbs from her hands. "If that were true, Chase wouldn't be in jail. He should have thought about Wyatt before he went on his revenge trip."

He opened his mouth to defend Chase, but he couldn't. "Well, he's paying dearly for it. His career is over, he's stuck in prison and he wants to see his kid."

He could just make out her eyebrows arching over the rim of her cup as she sipped her coffee.

"His wants are not as important as Wyatt's needs right now. Ask Wyatt if he wants to visit his dad. If he does, thoroughly prepare him on what to expect."

She made good points. Wyatt's needs were important. And he was starting to act like a normal ten-year-old again. Drew didn't want to set back his progress by traumatizing him with a prison visit. But he also didn't want to prevent his best friend from seeing his son. Lauren might think Chase was a loser, but Drew knew how much the man loved Wyatt.

"Thanks," he said. "I'll do that."

"Oh, and before I forget again, I think you should know Wyatt is determined to play football this summer."

"What?" His voice hardened. Couldn't one week go by without a new complication?

"Yep." She flourished her wrist. "Seems there are some *cool* kids playing, and one of their dads is coaching a team."

"Must be rec ball." He'd played at that age, too. It had been fun. A sport tailor-made for him. Sure, he'd made bad plays at times, but football had been his life. "I don't think the school district sponsors teams until seventh or eighth grade."

"Are you going to let him play?"

"I can't." He propped his elbows on the table. "If it was up to me, I'd sign him up. Let him learn about life himself. But Chase couldn't have been more clear on the topic."

"Could you ask him again?"

He shook his head. "I don't think so. I mean, I can try, but when he gets something in his head, watch out."

"Maybe you could sign Wyatt up for soccer or something else instead."

"Good idea." Chase hadn't said anything about soccer. "I'll check online later." He yawned. Overnights were exhausting. The middle-of-the-night calls had done him in.

"I'd better get out of here so you can have your beauty sleep." Lauren stacked the plates and stood.

"Leave them. I'll clean up."

Her lopsided smile sent a surge of energy through his body.

"I've got it," Lauren said. "Go to bed. I'll see you in a few days."

"Wait." He didn't want her to leave. Wanted to prolong each minute with her. But she was opening the patio door to go inside. "Won't I see you tomorrow?"

Turning back, she narrowed her eyes. "Why?"

"The pancake breakfast." She must have seen the signs around town or the ones plastered to the fire station door. "Aren't you coming?"

"Pancake breakfast? What are you talking about?"

"Our annual fund-raiser. It's at the station. Tickets are cheap. We've got fun and games. I'm sure you want to hop around in the bounce house." He plucked the plates out of her hand and slid the patio door open wider for her. "You should come."

"What time?"

"Seven to eleven."

"Can I bring a friend?"

A guy friend or a girl friend? He sighed. He had no right to ask. "Sure."

"I never miss the annual pancake breakfast." Megan adjusted her sundress straps.

"I always miss it." Lauren sidestepped two young boys chasing each other. What a silly thing to say. Of course she did—she'd lived in another state.

It felt good to go to a public event. The few times she'd ventured from her apartment outside of work or errands since moving back had been the Friday dinner with Drew and Wyatt at Uncle Joe's Restaurant and the visit to the station with Wyatt. For the first time in months, she actually wanted to be out and about. She couldn't deny she'd been smiling more now that Drew and Wyatt were in her life. She wondered if Drew had discussed visiting Chase with Wyatt.

"Something tells me you're here for more than the pancakes." Lauren followed Megan to the back of the line. The entire town must have shown up. An enormous white tent was set up on the lawn behind the station. Rows of tables and folding chairs were already full of families dining on sausage links and pancakes, and out on the lawn, two bounce houses jiggled in the light breeze. Tables with activities were set up beside them, and a playground and baseball diamond were a short distance away. "Do you think we'll find a spot to sit?"

"Oh, yeah. No problem. I've got this." Megan waved dismissively and leaned in. "I've had my eye on Ben Santos for a while now. See? Over there. The cutie serving sausages."

Lauren squinted. The line moved surprisingly fast. "Black hair? Tall?"

"That's him." Megan tipped her chin up and plastered her brightest smile on as they approached the food station. A female firefighter handed them both plates. "How's it going, Amanda?"

"Can't complain." The woman didn't seem overly thrilled to be there. "Ben and Stan will get you set up with hotcakes and sausages. Juice and coffee are on the table at the end."

They shuffled down the line, but Megan dug her heels in at the sausage station. "Hey, Ben."

"Well, hello, Megan." The man looked happier than a five-year-old skipping to an ice-cream truck. "It's good to see you."

"I always show up for a good cause." Megan twirled a section of hair around her finger.

Talk about obvious. The line behind Lauren was getting restless, but Ben seemed oblivious.

He set the tongs down, leaning over the warming tray. "I'm sure glad you did. Where you sitting?"

"It's pretty full." Megan shrugged, somehow making the gesture seem helpless. "I guess we could stand and eat, huh, Lauren?"

Lauren choked down a chortle at the overly disappointed tone in her voice. Megan should have been an actress. Was this Ben guy actually buying this?

"You can't eat standing up." All business, he straightened and gestured to another firefighter standing behind him. "Miggs, take over for me. Come with me, ladies." A minute later he escorted them to a side table where a few of the fire crew were taking a break. "Scoot over."

One of them grumbled, but at the sight of Megan and Lauren, they all quickly scooted down.

"Plenty of room. Right here." A man patted the bench and grinned at Lauren.

She was going to strangle Megan later. Ben and Megan had squished in at the other end of the table. Neither had eyes for anyone but each other.

"Actually, Lauren, there's a free spot next to me."

How had she not noticed Drew sitting at the end?

"Thanks, Drew." She sat next to him and spread a paper napkin across her lap. "Good turnout."

"Yeah, it is."

"Where's Wyatt?" A smear of butter and a hefty dose of syrup completed her hotcakes. She cut them and took a bite.

Drew straightened, turning his head to check the bounce house area. "He's off playing games with a few friends. I think one was named Levi."

"I'm glad he's comfortable enough to do that now.

This will be fun for him." The name Levi rang bells in her brain. Wasn't he one of the cool kids Wyatt mentioned?

"He stuck by me real close the first half hour. Boredom must have loosened him up enough to go with the boys."

"Did you have a chance to talk to him about playing football?"

He took a drink from a foam cup. "No, I had enough to deal with just discussing the possibility of visiting Chase."

She lowered her voice, not wanting everyone around them to hear. "So you talked about it then?"

"Yeah. He wants to go."

"Don't sound so excited."

"You made me think about it more. I'm worried it will be a lot to take in. Like you said, it might be scary for a young kid. Barbed wire, metal detectors. Is that good for him? I did a little research, though. One article said visiting an incarcerated parent helps a child maintain attachment and can get rid of some of the kid's fears about how the parent is doing in prison. What do you think?"

"Chase wants a relationship with Wyatt, and vice versa, so I say yes. Try a visit." She sopped up another bite with syrup. "Did you go over what to expect?"

Drew gazed off in the distance. "I did."

"And?"

"He still wants to go," Drew said. "He asked if you'd go with us."

She finished chewing. "Me?"

"I told him not to count on it." He averted his eyes.

"Why not? I'd be happy to drive with you. What facility is Chase in?" She'd been to prisons before. It didn't bother her any more than home visits in dangerous neighborhoods did. Not her favorite, but it was part of the job. She'd taken self-defense classes in her early twenties, always carried pepper spray and kept a pocketknife in her purse at all times. More important, she prayed for protection. She didn't live in an invincibility bubble, but she forged ahead anyhow.

"I didn't know how you'd feel about it, and I don't want you to feel obligated. You're already helping so much."

She waved her hand, scoffing. "I'm not doing much. Hanging out with a sweet kid like Wyatt isn't difficult. Tell me the date of the visit, and I'll come with you."

Drew filled her in on the specifics.

"I won't be allowed to go into the actual visitation room with him." Lauren set the used plastic silverware on her empty plate. "You guys can drop me off somewhere nearby while you visit. But let Wyatt know I'll be there for him before and after."

"The prison is two hours away. Are you sure you're up for it?"

"I'm up for it."

"Thank you." His eyes shone with gratitude. And something else.

A woman approached. She had a professional air about her, and unlike the rest of the people eating breakfast who wore casual clothes, she wore dress pants and a blouse.

"Excuse me. I'm sorry to interrupt, but are you Lauren Pierce?" She stood behind her and Drew. Lauren shifted in her seat to stare up at the woman while Drew excused himself to get another cup of coffee.

"I am."

"Susanne Gilbert, principal of Lake Endwell High. I talked to Joanna Mills yesterday."

That was quick. Lauren hadn't yet decided if she was going to apply for the counselor job. When she'd opened the online application file, icy tendrils had wrapped around her heart. She wasn't dumb. The job was more than transcripts and schedules. It was teen suicide, bullying and drug abuse. It was high school dropouts and cliques.

It was troubled kids desperately in need of help all over again.

She stood and shook the woman's hand. "Nice to meet you."

"I'd love to set up an interview with you. Joanna mentioned you'd be interested in coaching our cheerleaders."

"I am interested in coaching. I used to be a cheerleader here, and I really enjoyed it. I'm not sure about the counseling job, though."

"Why not apply? We can discuss the details over an interview. I have several other applicants, but given your background in Lake Endwell and your experience as a social worker... Well, let's just say I did some research and was impressed."

"Thank you." She wouldn't be so impressed if she knew Lauren's mistakes.

Principal Gilbert handed her a business card. "The link to the online application is on the back. Hope to hear from you soon."

Drew stood nearby. He held their empty paper plates in his hand. She couldn't read his face.

"So you're applying for a job?" He took a few steps in the direction of a large trash can. She joined him.

"I'm considering it. Cheerleading coach."

"And the counselor job Mrs. Gilbert mentioned?"

She shook her head. She couldn't go there. Not yet. Maybe not ever.

He tossed the plates in the can. "You'd be great at it."

"I don't know about that."

"You're good with Wyatt. Helping kids is in your blood." He strolled toward the bounce houses. In her blood? Her blood came from a drug addict and a murderer. Anything good inside her came from the Pierces and God. "For what it's worth, you're a natural. I think you should go for it."

"I'm researching a few other things." Like the cheer academy idea she'd all but abandoned. Or getting a safe and boring desk job. She grimaced.

He craned his neck to peer into the bounce houses. "Do you see Wyatt?"

She tried to look inside them but didn't recognize the kids. Slowly spinning in a circle, she checked the nearby park. "Isn't that him on the swings?"

"It sure is." Drew's eyes darkened as his jaw clenched. "I told him to tell me before going to the park. I'm going to have a word with him."

He strode in the park's direction. Lauren stayed and watched. A woman with a camera stood to the side of the playground, snapping several photos. What was she doing? Drew had told Lauren he hadn't had any issues with aggressive reporters since moving here.

He stopped to talk to the woman. By his posture, Lauren assumed he knew her. Probably a mom of one of the kids.

Overreacting. She'd been overreacting to her fears for months.

Lauren turned back to find Megan. The sun warmed her face, but her insides were chilled. She was glad

Drew took Wyatt's safety serious. A ten-year-old boy had no business running around without telling an adult where he was. On one hand, she wanted Drew to come down hard on him so he wouldn't do it again. But the other hand sympathized with Wyatt and wondered if she was making a big deal out of nothing.

Running off to a playground without telling Drew wasn't that big of a deal. But if it led to worse mistakes, like sneaking out in the middle of the night...

Discipline was worth the pain. If Jay would have gotten an ounce of discipline from his mother that week in December, he might have lived. And what about Treyvon? By the time she was assigned his and Jay's case, Treyvon had been fifteen with eyes wide-open about life. She had cared about him. Her heart squeezed at the thought of him in juvenile hall. Since quitting her job, she'd made no contact with him. He was no longer her case.

He might not be her case, but did that make him nothing to her?

Her conscience prodded. Maybe he *was* her case. Not as a social worker but as a human being who cared about him. Maybe it was time to contact him. Find out how he was doing.

Ask him to forgive her.

She dropped to a picnic table bench.

How could she ask him to forgive her when she hadn't really forgiven him?

She blamed him for Jay's death.

More than she blamed herself.

Oh, God, I'm sorry. I try not to think about it, but I'm so mad at that kid. Why did he join that awful gang and give in to their demands?

The day no longer seemed as bright. She needed

to go home and sit with Zingo until the urge to help Treyvon or apply for the counseling position passed.

Her heart wasn't ready for either.

Maybe a boring desk job was the way to go.

Chapter Seven

$\sim$

Bringing Wyatt to visit Chase was the right decision, wasn't it?

Drew studied the visitation room at the correctional facility. One wall was painted bright blue with a mural of fish. A bookcase with picture books and several tiny chairs were under it for small children. The rest of the room was filled with round tables with seating for two or three people. He, Wyatt and Chase sat at one of the tables. After the two-hour drive, they'd dropped Lauren off at a nearby mall before traveling the last few miles here.

"You doing better in school?" Chase had teared up initially at seeing Wyatt, but after a few sniffs and a quick wipe of his eyes, he'd gotten down to business. "Are you keeping up with math? Reading books?"

"School's done." Wyatt hugged his arms tightly around his body. "I don't need to read."

"You have to keep up with reading over the summer." Chase's eye twitched. "Drew will take you to the bookstore. Pick out some good books for you."

Wyatt glared, then averted his gaze.

"What was that look for?"

"Reading is boring. I'm playing football."

Drew could practically hear Wyatt completing the thought, *Just like you, Dad.*

"No. Absolutely not." Chase shook his head.

"That's not fair." Wyatt brought his hands, balled into fists, on the table. "Levi wants me on his team. His dad is the coach. It's flag football. I won't get hurt."

Drew exchanged a charged look with Chase and gave his head a slight shake.

"We can talk about it more later, Wyatt," Drew said. "Why don't you tell your dad about yesterday's end-of-school-year picnic?"

Wyatt sighed, answering Chase's questions in monosyllables. Maybe coming here was a mistake. Drew would do about anything to talk to Lauren right now. He needed advice. Or reassurance. Maybe both. But he'd had to check in his phone at the front desk when they arrived. He and Wyatt had signed in and gone through the security procedure with the other visitors. Wyatt had grown quieter with each passing minute, and his discomfort seeped around him like a bubble full of jelly. Drew could have reached out and touched it.

"Lauren and I are going to play tennis next week. I've never tried it before, but I'm pretty sure I'll beat her..."

Drew raised his eyebrows at that one. At least Wyatt was talking without the huge chip on his shoulder.

"So this Lauren, you like spending time with her?" Chase's smile was tender as he listened to Wyatt.

"Yeah. She's awesome. But she listens to awful music."

"You'll have to introduce her to George Strait." Chase grinned at Wyatt, who grinned right back. "Show her some good music, right?"

"Yeah." Wyatt grew serious. "Are you doing okay here, Dad?" His forehead creased in worry.

Chase blinked. "Well, uh, it's not bad. I have a schedule, kind of like with football. I do things at certain times, and I work out. I have time to read, too."

"You're reading on purpose?" Wyatt grimaced. "Why?"

"I'm filling my mind with good stuff. All those years playing football were busy. I never took the time to slow down. I've got time on my hands now, and I've got questions."

Wyatt looked confused.

"The books I'm reading are helping me answer some of those questions."

Wyatt chewed on his bottom lip.

"Wyatt, will you do one thing for me while we're apart?"

He stared expectantly at Chase.

"Fill your mind with good stuff." Chase's chest expanded, and he leaned back in his chair. "I'm praying for you. Keep going to church. Listen to Drew. And put in some George Strait for Lauren."

"I wish you were coming home with us, Dad." Wyatt's face fell. "Then I could play football and—"

"You're not playing football. Period. End of story."

The guard announced the visit was over. Chase looked emotional as they left. Wyatt didn't make a peep until they finished their paperwork and were halfway to the mall to meet Lauren.

"It's not fair," Wyatt said.

"What isn't fair?" Drew ached to pull over and hold Wyatt, but the boy's stiff-as-a-steel-rod posture probably wasn't ready to accept a hug. He didn't blame the kid. Visiting the prison had been difficult for him, too, and he was a grown man. Between the guards stopping them on their way into the parking lot, the metal detectors, pat down, sign-in process, limited contact and strict rules throughout the visit, Drew felt completely and utterly exhausted.

"Why does Dad have to be in jail? He didn't do anything wrong."

"He did do something wrong, Wyatt."

"I would have done the same thing."

"I hope not."

Wyatt stuck his bottom lip out and turned away to face the window.

"Look, that wasn't easy, going to see him. It will be easier next time."

"I'm not going back."

Drew's stomach dropped. "Why not?"

"He wouldn't even listen. He doesn't care. I wish I could live with you forever, Uncle Drew." The last words were practically spat out.

Drew scratched his head. Why would Wyatt feel that way? Drew thought the visit had gone pretty well, all things considered.

"He cares about you." Drew kept his tone low. "He loves you."

When Wyatt didn't respond, he tried to figure out what to say to get through to him. He couldn't shake the feeling his quest to make life normal for Wyatt had just taken two enormous steps back. Thankfully, the mall entrance was up ahead. Maybe Lauren would have some insight in how to fix this. Whatever it was.

Lauren tapped her fingernails against her empty smoothie cup and stretched to see if Drew and Wyatt had arrived. Drew had texted her ten minutes earlier to say they were on their way. The sitting area in the center of the mall had comfortable faux leather chairs and was filled with busy shoppers.

She had a bad feeling about the visit. The first time was always hard on kids. As much as she didn't want the inconvenient feelings of caring about Wyatt, she had them. She cared deeply about him. And she knew he was hurting. She just knew it.

As soon as she spotted Drew's dark cropped hair above the crowd, she weaved through the shoppers on her way to them. Even fifteen feet away Wyatt looked pale and miserable. Her chest tightened. How she wanted to take his pain from him.

Not caring about the people trying to get through the aisles, she stopped directly in front of Drew and took Wyatt in her arms. She held him tightly, kissing the top of his head. He melted into her arms, his small shoulders shaking as he began to cry.

She met Drew's eyes over Wyatt's head. She mouthed, "Give him a minute." He nodded. Drew's face was taut, his easygoing manner nowhere to be found. The visit must have done a number on both of them.

Chase, you stupid jerk. If you only knew what you did to these two. I want to wring your neck.

"It's okay, Wyatt," she whispered, holding him tightly. She'd never let him go. "It's okay."

He sniffled and, keeping his head down, tried to wipe his eyes. *Poor baby.* Probably was afraid to let Drew see his tears. Tears of her own sprang up. Why did kids have to have parents in jail? *Why?*

"Come on, honey. Let's go somewhere private." She straightened, keeping her arm around him, and led him toward the entrance of an upscale store. She'd scoped it out earlier. They rode the escalator in silence with

Drew behind them, and she took them to the corner, where a nice restroom and lounge were tucked away. She kept Wyatt close to her on a sofa, and Drew sat in a chair across from them.

"You were brave today, Wyatt." She took his hand in hers and squeezed. He leaned his head against her upper arm. "I mean it. It takes a strong person to visit a prison."

Drew cleared his throat. "You would have been proud of him, Lauren. He didn't flinch when the guards patted us down."

"Well, that wasn't a big deal." Wyatt sat up. Lauren wanted to tuck his head back on her arm, but she was glad he seemed to be recovering. Instrumental music played softly around them, and the scent of lilac from the nearby candle section filled the air.

"It is a big deal," she said. "I'm guessing Drew begged them not to touch him. He probably swatted their hands away."

"Guilty." He grinned, but it didn't quite reach his eyes. "I don't like people patting me down."

"I don't, either." Wyatt folded his hands in his lap. "I wish…"

Drew's mouth tightened into a thin line.

"What?" Lauren prodded.

"I wish he wasn't in jail."

"I wish he wasn't, either," she said.

"He doesn't even care."

Drew opened his mouth, but she shook her head as nicely as possible to cut him off.

"About what?" She kept her voice quiet, soothing.

"About me. He won't let me play football. He doesn't care I only got to see him for a little bit and twenty billion people were in the room. He doesn't care we don't play video games. I miss our old house."

Wyatt's body throbbed with pent-up anger. She feared touching him would make him snap, sending him into a million pieces.

"He cares," Drew said. "Trust me when I say he would do anything to live with you and play video games and hang out with you again. He just can't."

"Drew's right, Wyatt, but you still have every right to be angry about it."

Wyatt dropped his face in his hands, and his body shook with quiet sobs. Lauren wrapped her arms around him. "It's okay. Let it out."

As she held him, Drew stalked to the archway. If Wyatt's demeanor screamed "shattered," Drew's shouted "in over my head and angry about it." He thrust his hands in the pockets of his jeans and rocked back on his heels, a grim expression on his face.

Lauren reached into her purse and grabbed a tissue. She handed it to Wyatt, and he wiped his eyes and blew his nose. When he seemed like he had himself together, she tipped his chin up with her hand and looked into his eyes.

"I'm glad you're not holding it in."

He nodded.

"Remember, it's good to cry when you're sad. When you're ready, why don't we go somewhere fun to eat?" She tilted her head to see what Drew thought about her proposition. His lips parted and he nodded.

"Your choice, Wyatt."

Wyatt wiped his nose one last time and threw the tissue away.

Lauren took a deep breath. *Thank You, Lord, for let-*

*ting me be here today. Thank You for letting me be part
of his life, even if it's only for a few months.*

"Do they have a Dave & Buster's here?" Wyatt asked.

"Dave & Buster's it is."

Three hours later Drew checked the rearview mirror.
Wyatt had fallen asleep. After pizza and more games
than Drew could count, they'd hit the road to drive
home. The sun descended bright and beautiful in the
sky, a welcome reminder of God's daily blessings.

"I can't begin to thank you." He glanced at Lauren.
"Thank you. Thank you."

"I should be thanking you. I was glad I could be there
for him." Her sweet smile landed right in his heart. Even
across the seats he could smell her tropical perfume.

"I'm so far in your debt it's not even funny." He
shook his head, feeling lighter than he had all day. "How
did you know how to handle him? I had no idea what
to say. He was so mad when we left the prison, and
I thought the visit went pretty well. Shows you how
much I know."

"I'm sure the visit did go fine." She shifted to face
him. "Seeing your parent in jail brings out emotions
you have no control over. It's not something most people have to do. It's confusing."

He hadn't really thought of it that way. He turned the
volume of the country station down to hear her better.
"Well, he claims he's not going back to visit again."

Traffic on I-94 hedged them in, forcing Drew to
slow until a semi passed. What if Wyatt refused to
visit Chase? The caseworker might not let Chase have
custody when he was released. It would be a crime for
Wyatt and his dad to be separated longer than necessary.

Lauren faced him. "Was it awkward between Chase

and Wyatt? Did they seem uncomfortable? What was their conversation like?"

Impressions of the visitation room came to mind. Unspoken emotions had bounced off every person in there, including him. "We all sat at a table. Chase wants Wyatt to read more."

She chuckled. "I'm sure he took that well."

"Yeah, right. He doesn't see the point in reading." He grinned, glancing her way. Man, she was pretty. *Eyes on the road, Gannon.* "He mentioned football, and Chase barely let him finish. It was just no, and that was it."

"Wyatt probably didn't like that."

"Nope."

"Anything else?"

"Not really. We talked about normal stuff. Nothing newsworthy."

She brightened. "I'm guessing Wyatt's reaction was pure nerves. Maybe some anger mixed in. He'll change his mind about visiting Chase. It might take time, though. Are you willing to wait?"

"I'll wait as long as I need to. Wyatt and Chase were always close. I don't want that to change." The vehicles were driving at a normal speed again, allowing him to relax his grip on the steering wheel. "You know a lot about this. Did you visit your dad in jail?"

"No. I have no memories of him."

No memories of her father? He frowned. "So I'm assuming when he went to jail your parents adopted you?"

"Not quite." Her gaze remained level. "Apparently, my birth mother raised me until she died—I was three at the time—and then I went to foster homes."

Homes. Plural. The conversation was starting to bother him, but he needed to know more.

"How many are we talking about?"

She drew her knee up and rested her chin on it, tilting her head slightly. "Five."

"Five?" He hadn't meant to bark. "Why so many?"

Her smile faded. "The first was temporary because I had nowhere to go when my mom died of an overdose. I think I was there a few months. I don't remember. The next one I lived in for two years, but they had twins and another baby on the way, and I guess it was too much. I didn't live at number three for long. And number four wasn't a good fit, but they were friends with the Pierces, so it worked out for the best."

"When did they adopt you?"

"I was seven." Her face grew pensive. "Do you remember the day we walked to City Park? You told me about college."

He nodded.

"That afternoon I went to my closet to look for a file. I found my old duffel bag. It's stained, ripped and purple."

Where was she going with this? Who cared about an old purple bag?

She continued, "My earliest memories are of shoving all my clothes, every tiny thing I owned—and I didn't own much—into that bag each night."

"Why did you do that?"

"I never knew when a social worker would show up and take me to a new home. It took me over a year of living with the Pierces before I trusted them enough to unpack it."

It was as if someone had shot staples into his chest. Hard to imagine the amazing woman next to him as a child so prepared to move constantly she'd kept a packed bag. "That's terrible, Lauren."

"It's why I am who I am. I wanted to help kids like

me. But…" She shrugged. "Guess that didn't work out so great, either. I think I'll always be the little girl with a packed bag, waiting to be shuffled off to another home."

If an exit or rest stop had been nearby, he would have taken it. This wasn't a conversation for his truck. He wanted to comfort her, hold her. But the cars whizzing past kept his hands planted on the wheel.

"You're so much more than a little girl getting shuffled off. You see that, don't you?"

She stared out the front windshield, her shoulder lifting slightly.

"You understood what Wyatt needed today."

"Anyone would have done the same."

"That's not true. I wish you'd stop doing that," he said. "Wyatt needed you today—I needed you today—and you came through for us. That matters. It matters to me."

"Don't count on me, Drew. I might not be there next time."

He ignored her words, catching the fear clouding her gray eyes. He'd asked a lot of her ever since moving back to Lake Endwell, and he hadn't given much back in return.

What did he have to give? He'd admired his memories of her, but the adult Lauren next to him was more—so much more—than he'd imagined.

He didn't have anything she needed, but he could give her his friendship. With no strings attached. Good for life. No matter what, he would be there for her if she needed him.

"Lauren, I will never forget what you've done—what you're doing—for Wyatt." *And for me.* "I care about you, and I never want you to feel like that little girl with the duffel bag again. I'm here for you. Whatever you need, I'll be here."

Her throat moved as she swallowed.

"I don't need—"

"I know what you're doing." He glanced over at her. "You can push me away all you want, but I'm here for you. Always. That's a promise, and I'm not budging."

He was falling for her. He knew it. He wasn't stupid enough to think he had a chance with her, but her friendship meant a lot to him. And he *would* do everything in his power to make sure she never felt unwanted again.

Chapter Eight

"I never expected Drew Gannon to be so..." Lauren searched for the right word and set a plate in front of Megan before sitting across from her the next evening. The windows in her apartment were open to let the breeze inside. Zingo looked up at her and meowed. The cat thought he wanted people food, but every time she offered, he turned up his nose and stalked away, tail high. *Picky thing.*

"Sooo...what?" Megan rubbed her hands together and eyed the chicken Caesar salad Lauren had thrown together.

"So understanding. And patient." Lauren fluffed the salad with tongs. She kept seeing his kind eyes. The way he'd tried so hard to make Wyatt feel better playing games at the restaurant. Then there was his profile—handsome, strong—in the truck last night. And his words... Her heartbeat sped up. "He really surprises me."

"Ben said he's great to work with. Humble but not afraid to take charge. A lot of the guys look up to him, not that they'll stop ribbing him anytime soon."

"I could see why they would think that." She chewed a bite of the salad.

"Am I sensing a romance?" Megan waggled her eyebrows.

"No. I'm helping Wyatt. Just for the summer." But Drew's promise had replayed in her mind roughly a thousand times since he'd said it last night. Could someone make a promise like that? No matter how much she pushed him away, he'd always be there for her? As much as the thought filled her with hope, she was realistic. She pushed people away for their own good. Including Drew.

"Mmm-hmm." Megan bit into a crouton. "Yum. This is so good."

"Thanks. I made the croutons myself." Lauren enjoyed playing around with recipes. She hadn't had the time or energy to cook much in Chicago. "How is it going with Ben?"

"We went to a movie yesterday. He invited me to dinner next week."

"Sounds promising."

"Yeah, I like him." Megan grinned. "We should double date sometime. You and Drew and me and Ben."

Lauren lifted her gaze to the ceiling. "I'm not dating Drew."

"Why not? He's supercute, seems to like you and he's available."

And he'd unwittingly gotten her to tell him things she'd never told before. Things he could use against her. Scary things. He might say she couldn't push him away, but he was wrong. At some point he'd add up everything she'd revealed, and she wouldn't have to push him away. He'd leave on his own, and then where would she be?

Not heartbroken—not if she could help it.

She needed to get Megan off this topic, pronto. "What do you think about me as the varsity cheerleading coach?"

Megan dropped her fork. "I think it would be fabulous! Did you apply for the job or something?"

"No, not yet. Joanna told me I'd have a better shot at it if I worked for the school. And I chatted with Principal Gilbert at the pancake breakfast while you were making googly-eyes at Ben. She's interested in interviewing me for a guidance counselor position."

"Well, there you go." Megan threw her hands up as if the solution was obvious. "You'd be an amazing counselor, and you'd be an awesome cheer coach. Isn't it great how this worked out?"

"Whoa there, lady." Lauren stabbed a forkful of lettuce. "I haven't applied for either job, and who knows if I would get them?"

"*I* know. This is ideal. Please tell me you're considering. After dinner, we should go through the application."

Lauren had to admit both jobs appealed to her. Lake Endwell was safe and tame compared with Chicago. The teenagers she'd be working with wouldn't be recruited to gangs or shot dead on the sidewalk two blocks from their homes.

"I guess it couldn't hurt to apply. It's not as if I have to take the job. And she might hire someone else."

"Right." Megan's knowing smile made her chuckle.

"I know you think it's a done deal, but my life usually doesn't work that way."

"We'll see about that."

Lauren had discussed the position with her mom earlier in the afternoon. Mom and Dad thought she'd be smart to apply and that the job would suit her. But she hadn't confided all her fears to them. They knew she'd left Chicago because of the boys, but she hadn't told them everything. How guilty she felt about it.

Megan pointed her fork at Lauren. "You have all these credentials, and you're great at knowing what to do or say when anyone is going through a rough time. I'd love to see you using your talents—all of them—right here in Lake Endwell."

The backs of Lauren's eyes prickled. Megan thought all that? "I have no plans to leave Lake Endwell. When I moved back it felt like I was taking the easy way out, trying to escape my mistakes, but I knew being close to Mom and Dad would help me recover, and I was right. Now I can't imagine not living near them. And I have to admit while I'm enjoying my time off when I'm not with Wyatt, it's getting boring. I definitely need a new career."

"Good." Megan reached over and squeezed her hand. "Let's get a résumé together and fill out the application."

How many years had she longed for good friends like Megan and Drew? And now she had them.

If Drew meant what he said...

He might have good intentions, but he could turn out to be a seasonal friend.

She hoped not. She'd have to wait and see.

"Gannon. You're riding with Ludlow on the LSV today." Chief Reynolds barked out everyone's duties Tuesday morning, and they dispersed.

Drew wished his probation period was over so he could drive the ambulance again. He and Tony usually didn't talk much, but he could sense a grudging acceptance from him. As for the other firefighters, Drew still heard a lot of stupid comments about failing at college football or someone droning on about the good old days playing for Lake Endwell High. He'd conditioned himself not to respond.

Sometimes he felt as though the only people who really knew him were Chase and Lauren.

"I'll be in the supply room if you need me." Tony hitched his chin toward the door at the end of the hall.

"Sounds good. I'm going to knock out a few things on my list." Drew went upstairs to the weight room.

He'd talked to Chase last night. Wyatt had refused to come out of his room for the phone call. Drew had to break it to Chase that Wyatt was upset after the visit. The silence on the other line had stabbed at him, but eventually Chase had begun talking. He'd told Drew he'd been thinking about his life a lot and all the mistakes he'd made. He was studying the Bible, and he'd broken his silence with the press to talk to a reporter from *People* magazine. He wanted other people to learn from his mistakes.

That was good and all, but it didn't exactly help Wyatt out now. The kid had barely talked or eaten the past two days. It was as if Wyatt had reverted back to the withdrawn boy Drew had driven into town.

Drew stretched his neck from side to side to loosen the building tension. He'd better call Lauren and find out if she was faring any better with Wyatt.

He could still see her big smile in his truck the other day. She'd revealed so much—more than he ever expected—and he meant what he'd told her. He owed her and not in a let's-get-this-over-with-and-let-me-pay-you way. He owed her for trusting him when she had no reason to. For giving Wyatt the comfort Drew hadn't realized he needed. For being generous with her time and emotions even though it cost her.

He now knew how much caring about other people cost her.

And he was falling for her because of it.

Alarms beeped through the speakers. Listening to the call, he ran down the stairs to the ambulance. Pulled on his gear as Tony joined him. They both listened to the directions and prepared to leave. Chest pains, possible heart attack. Didn't sound good.

"I know that address." Tony's voice hardened. "My uncle lives there."

"Then we'd better get there quickly." Drew mentally prepared as Tony drove the fastest route available. "Can you handle this?"

"I'm on this call for a reason."

"We'll take care of him. Is he married?"

"Yeah, Aunt Luann is probably a wreck."

"Are you sure you're okay? I know this is your uncle, and you're probably tempted to take the lead."

"It's my uncle. I should take the lead." His face reddened.

"No. We stick to the plan. You're going to have to trust me. If anything goes wrong, you can blame me forever, but I've been doing this for almost ten years. I'm just saying I'm detached." Drew raised his eyebrows. The address was a few miles away.

"Okay. Gannon, so help me—"

"You can kill me. I get it." Drew nodded grimly. This was about more than being accepted in Fire Station 4, although Tony's feelings toward him teetered on the edge of a cliff. The next hour would determine the fate of Tony's uncle's life. *God, I need Your help. Help us save this man.*

* * *

"What interests you?" Lauren dragged her finger along the spines of the middle-grade books at Lake Endwell Library. The scent of magazine pages and old books filled the air. She hadn't seen Wyatt since the prison visit. So far the day had been full of monosyllables, shrugs and mopey looks. Everything in her yelled to ask him how he was feeling now that it had been a few days since visiting Chase, but she knew better than to push. At least not yet.

"Nothing here." Wyatt scuffed his toe on the carpet, his face as sullen as his voice.

"Nothing interests you? Not one thing?" She straightened, crossing her arms over her chest and tapping her foot. "That is just sad."

Nothing really interested her here, either. She wasn't much of a reader, but she wasn't about to tell Wyatt that.

Her thoughts kept returning to her future. She and Megan had spent a few hours last night working on the online application for the high school counselor position. But she hadn't pressed Send. Couldn't. Not yet.

Maybe not ever.

She didn't know if working with teens and all their complexities would be wise. Every time she told herself Lake Endwell was different, the reality of teen problems—bullying and suicide and broken families— filled her mind.

"What about an adventure novel?" She selected a book about pirates. "This seems interesting."

He refused to look at it.

"Oh, I've got it. Perfect for you." She held up a pink book with a princess on the cover. Wyatt's glare could have frozen a fiery comet. "Okay. Maybe not. Do you like comics? They have graphic novels. Or magazines?"

"I'm not reading. Just because *he* wants me to doesn't mean I have to."

Ahh... That *he* was as loaded as the baked potato she'd piled high with toppings for lunch. Chase.

"You don't want to read because your dad wants you to?"

"I don't have to listen to him. He's not here."

Lauren weighed her options. Wyatt wasn't in the right mental state to get books, and he clearly needed to discuss his feelings about his dad. "Come on—let's get out of here and get ice cream."

"Finally." He zoomed straight to the entrance.

Out in the warm sun, robins flew back and forth between the lawn and trees along the sidewalk. She strolled in the direction of JJ's Ice Cream three blocks away. Green grass lined the sidewalks. It felt good to be wearing shorts and walking outside on a beautiful summer Michigan day. If only the conflicted boy next to her could catch some of that feeling, too…but that would be doubtful considering the conversation she needed to have with him.

"Why don't you think you should have to listen to your dad?" She kept her tone even and her gaze straight ahead.

"He's not here." His legs marched next to hers, and she inwardly sighed at the pent-up anger punctuating each step.

"No, he's not. He still loves you, though. He's your dad."

"Some dad," he said under his breath. It went straight to her heart. She knew. She'd been on the merry-go-round of emotions about her biological parents count-less times growing up. They reached a small public area with a shaded lawn, benches and a fountain surrounded by pink-and-purple flowers.

"Let's sit here a minute." She took a seat on the bench facing the fountain.

"I thought we were getting ice cream."

"We will." Lauren patted the spot next to her. The water gurgled, and tall oaks towered over the area. Wyatt dropped onto the bench. She tipped her head and smiled at him. "You're mad at him, huh?"

"No, I don't care." He made it sound as if his dad being incarcerated made no difference to him.

"I think you do. It's okay to be mad. He let you down."

"He did not!" Wyatt glared up at her with a glint of vulnerability in his eyes. "He had to do it."

"What did he have to do?" She knew what he was alluding to, but she wanted him to verbalize it.

He reached down and picked a blade of grass, smashing it in his fingers.

"Wyatt, I want to hear you say it."

The grass dropped from his hand. "He had to get even with that guy."

Lauren weighed her options. Wyatt's one-track mind made sense to her, but his actions conflicted with what he said. If she pointed it out to him, he'd get defensive. Maybe she could guide him to the truth without stating it.

"What if he hadn't gone after him?" She watched his reaction. His legs were bent so the toes of his athletic shoes just touched the sidewalk under the bench.

"He had to."

"What if he hadn't?" Should she keep pushing?

His skinny knees bounced under his basketball shorts. "Len would have gotten away with it."

"What if Chase had contacted the police with Len's whereabouts instead of going after him?"

His little jaw shifted. "Then we'd still be in Detroit, and we'd live together, and I wouldn't have to visit him in prison. I'd see him every day. I'd be playing with my friends and going to my old school."

"You miss all that. I don't blame you," she said. "Your dad made a choice, and you got hurt by it."

"He did it for my mom."

"And what about you?" she asked quietly.

"I would have gone after him, too." Wyatt turned away from her. For a minute she thought she'd gotten through to him, but he wasn't ready. Maybe it gave him comfort to cling to the idea his dad *had* to take the law into his own hands.

Lord, please open Wyatt's heart to the truth. Let him see and accept his dad made a mistake.

"Well, we all make choices. Sometimes we make the right ones, and sometimes we make the wrong ones."

"He made the right one."

"Did he? Making the right choice isn't always easy."

"How do we know what's right and what isn't?"

Lauren hesitated. "Does Drew take you to church?"

"Yes." His stomach gurgled.

"Let's talk while we walk." She stood again, and they strolled in the direction of the ice-cream shop. "Tell me what you know from going to church."

"Dad and Uncle Drew always say your heart knows the right thing to do. Your conscience tells you when you're doing the wrong thing."

"That's true. Your conscience guides you."

"And Dad and Uncle Drew told me being loyal is important."

"Yes, it is. But being loyal and blindly agreeing with

someone's actions aren't the same things. You know it's normal to be mad at your dad, right? I was mad a lot before my parents adopted me."

"I'm not mad."

"Are you sure about that?" She stepped over a raised crack in the sidewalk. "I'd be mad if I couldn't see my dad every day. Or if I had to go to a correctional facility to see him."

"I thought you didn't get to see your dad every day. He was in prison. Did you visit him, too?"

"I was talking about my adoptive dad. My real dad—no, I never met him." They stopped at a crosswalk until the traffic light changed. "Your dad loves you, Wyatt. My real dad never wanted me. Your dad does. He loves you."

Wyatt stared across the street, and the color drained from his face.

"What's wrong?" She kneeled and put her hands on his shoulders. "Wyatt, are you okay?"

He blinked, his mouth opening and shutting. She checked back over her shoulder and saw a man with a camera jogging around the corner of the dentist office, where bushes swayed. Had that man just taken their picture? She thought back to what Wyatt and Drew had said about reporters.

Fury boiled her blood. How dare they? How could anyone sneak around and hide to take an innocent little kid's picture? Weren't there laws about this?

If there weren't, there should be.

"Come on." She held his hand tightly. "You do not have to worry about some jerk taking your picture. Not if I have anything to say about it."

"Wh-what are you going to do?" His voice shook, and his fingers seemed so small in hers.

"First, we're going to the police. Then we're telling your uncle Drew."

Wyatt wrapped his arms around her waist and hugged her as if he never wanted to let her go. She stroked his hair, her heart hurting that some insensitive photographer would prey on a wounded child to make a buck.

"It's okay, Wyatt. You're safe with me."

He looked up at her through scared eyes and whispered, "Thanks."

She leaned down and kissed the top of his head. How could she make a statement like that? *You're safe with me?* What if he wasn't?

She'd have to do everything in her power to back that statement up.

I don't have to do this alone.

For months her prayers had been sporadic. Sure, she'd prayed for Wyatt a few minutes ago, but how long had it been since she'd opened her Bible? Attended church? She might pray now and then, but she wanted more.

And right now she needed power. God's power.

This was for Wyatt, and she refused to let him down. *Lord, please protect Wyatt from predators and give me the strength and wisdom to protect him, too.*

Drew leaned his forehead against his forearm propped against the wall in the locker room. This morning felt an eternity away. When they'd arrived at Tony's uncle's house, the man had shown clear signs of a heart attack, but he was alive. Drew immediately went to work. They followed protocol, stabilizing him and getting him to the emergency room in record time. Last they'd heard he was recovering from an emergency angioplasty. Tony had stayed at the hospital with his aunt, and the station had called Amanda to fill in for him.

He wanted to drop on the couch and forget today had ever happened.

It had been packed with one call after the other, including a minor car accident and an interior fire, where he'd treated an elderly woman for smoke inhalation. The firefighters had gotten her out quickly, but she'd been unconscious. He and Amanda had done everything in their power to clear her airways and get her breathing, but she'd been pronounced dead at the hospital.

An electrical short. A seventy-eight-year-old woman.

He couldn't make sense of it. The fire department had gotten to the scene within minutes. The search-and-rescue unit made it in and out with no problems. Her 1940s bungalow had survived with minor damage.

Why had she died?

Why hadn't he and Amanda been able to save her?

"Drew, there's someone here to see you." One of the guys stood in the doorway of the locker room.

"Be right there." He rubbed his face with both hands, straightened and took a deep breath. He tried to clear his head as he strode down the hall, but the woman's sunken cheeks, closed eyes and frail body hooked up to oxygen kept invading his thoughts.

He'd failed that woman.

Lauren stood in the kitchen, a lighthouse against a stormy sea. Without a thought, he closed the distance between them and took her in his arms. He held her tightly, pressing his cheek against her soft golden hair.

"What happened, Drew?" Her concern drove through his muddled brain, forcing him to step back. Reluctantly he let her go.

"It was a hard day." Pressing his finger and thumb

into the bridge of his nose, he scrambled to get his emotions in line. *Get it together, Gannon.* "Why are you here?"

"You look awful." Lauren ran her hand down his arm. "I wouldn't bother you, but... Is this a good time to talk? Or is that allowed?"

He looked at his watch. Almost five. "Now's a good time." Only then did he realize Wyatt wasn't there. "Where's Wyatt?"

"He's at my parents' house."

Drew gently took her arm and led her down the hall and outside to a nearby bench. "What's going on?"

"Wyatt and I were walking from the library, and we saw a man with a camera across the street." She sat and shifted to face him.

Her words filled his gut with dread. "I take it he wasn't a tourist?"

She shook her head and tendrils of hair escaped her ponytail, framing her face. "Tourists don't usually creep around the bushes of the dentist office."

Things clicked into place. Chase hadn't talked to the press in months, but the fact that he was speaking to *People* magazine had probably gotten leaked, bringing out the bottom-of-the-pond suckers who made their living taking pictures to sell to tabloids. He brought both hands to the back of his head and leaned back, trying not to freak out. "And Wyatt? He saw the guy?"

She nodded.

"Then what?"

"He was shaken up. We marched to the police station, and I talked to an officer." Her gray eyes grew darker than storm clouds, and her pretty chin tipped up. "If you think I'm going to let some scumbag prey on Wyatt, you are wrong. You should have seen his face, Drew.

He was terrified. I can't stop fantasizing about finding that guy and slapping him upside the head and telling him exactly how I feel—" Her eyes widened, and she frowned. She lowered her voice. "Sorry. Got carried away there. I'm just not putting up with anyone scaring Wyatt. He has enough to deal with."

All Lauren's righteous indignation drove out the defeat he'd been feeling earlier. He not only liked this warrior side of her; he needed it. Needed her strength right now. With her flushed cheeks and flashing eyes, he could picture her confronting a photographer. He could almost feel sorry for the guy if it ever happened.

"*You* are terrifying." He dragged his gaze from her lips.

Chin high, she sniffed. "Are you making fun of me?"

His lips curved upward. Her nervous glance his way only made his grin grow. "I'm not. I'm admiring you."

"Well, don't." Her back stiffened all prim and proper. One little tug and she'd be in his arms. What a mistake that would be. He had to stop thinking about her in a more-than-a-babysitter way.

"What did the police say?" His voice sounded husky, and he didn't care. He knew what she was going to say—he'd been to the police many times on Wyatt's behalf.

She folded her leg so the knee was on the bench between them. Her face grew animated. "Get this. They told me there isn't anything they can technically do. It's legal for anyone to take Wyatt's picture when we're out in public. I told the officer that was the stupidest thing I'd ever heard. I asked about stalking laws and privacy and you name it." She rolled her eyes.

"Thank you." Her hand was on her knee, and he took it in his, tracing her thumb.

"For what? I'm so frustrated. I mean, what are you supposed to do? Keep him chained in the house? At least the police were willing to help a little bit."

He frowned, confused. The police hadn't been willing to help him back in Detroit.

"The sheriff is friends with my dad. He'll let us know if anyone sees any suspicious people hanging around town."

Ahh...that makes sense. Drew patted her hand. "It's the tourist season. There will be a lot of people hanging around town."

Lauren sighed. "I know. But it's something."

"You did good." He wanted to close the inches between them and hold her. Not in a brotherly or thankful way. No, her maternal-lioness instincts attracted him, made him want to be in her protective circle. Not that he needed protecting—it just was great having someone care enough to fight on Wyatt's behalf, too. "You are the strongest woman I've ever met."

His words were out before he thought them through. They were true. But was it wise to put them out there?

Lauren's lips opened slightly as she mulled over them. To his disappointment, she withdrew her hand.

"I'd better get over to my parents'." She uncurled her legs, and he rose with her.

More than air stood between them. Awkwardness. Attraction.

He wasn't ready for it. He doubted she even felt it.

It was time to reclaim his role. To be strong. "Thanks, Lauren, for telling me and for going to the police. Don't worry. I'll take care of it. Nothing's going to happen to Wyatt."

Her shy smile warmed him. She turned, strolling to the sidewalk leading to the parking lot. Once she was safely in her car, he went back inside. A group of guys, including Ben, stood around in the kitchen.

"I wish Lauren Pierce would drop by to see me sometime."

"Like she'd ever look twice at you, Miggs."

This was usually where Drew buried his irritation and pasted on a grin to show them all he was a good sport. Not today. He just couldn't do it today.

"A photographer was snooping around town taking pictures of Wyatt." His voice sounded loud and harsh even to his ears.

A hush fell over the kitchen.

"What are you going to do about it?" Ben asked, widening his stance.

"There's not much I can do. It's not illegal for them to take his picture if he's out in public. We had to deal with this in Detroit, too. It's one of the reasons I moved back here."

Ben pushed his chest out, cracked his knuckles and looked dead serious. "Taking pictures might not be illegal, but that doesn't mean we have to roll out the welcome mat for anyone bothering the kid."

"That's right," Miggs said. "I'll ask my cousin Marie to let me know if anyone starts nosing around the Daily Donut."

"And we'll put the word out to our friends and families," Ben said. "I have two sisters. They know everything around here. If they hear about someone snapping pictures of him, we'll know within three seconds."

Drew fought back emotion. All of these guys who'd given him such a hard time since his first day had his back. They were his brothers. He could depend on them.

"I won't forget this." He made eye contact with each of them.

"You'd do the same for us."

"I would. Anything."

An ordinary day had gone from bad to worse, but the past ten minutes had blessed him unexpectedly.

Thank You, God, for sending me help. Lauren. My coworkers. I don't deserve it, but I'm thankful for them.

Chapter Nine

Sunday morning Lauren arrived early at church to gather her thoughts. She found a seat and soaked in the quiet peace. The space was bright and smelled of flowers and wood polish. Welcoming. Comforting. Exactly what she needed.

The past four days had been quiet. No one had seen any photographers around town, and for that she was glad. She'd finally pressed Send on the online application to be a high school counselor. Every time she thought about it, her stomach got upset, though. She'd purposely put it out of her mind as much as possible. But there were two things she couldn't get out of her mind no matter how hard she tried.

Drew. And Treyvon.

She had no idea why she couldn't get Treyvon off her mind. She'd been drawn more to Jay. Hadn't known Treyvon all that well. But he pressed against her heart more and more…

Then there was Drew. Why her brain fixated on him wasn't a mystery. He devoted his life to helping others. He loved Wyatt. He was spectacularly gorgeous.

He'd told her about how his coworkers at the station

had rallied around him to protect Wyatt. What a blessing to have a community to rely on in times like this. And Drew made her feel special, like she was better than she believed. It was a heady feeling.

Lauren crossed one leg over the other. She didn't trust feelings like that. Oh, she trusted Drew. How could she not? But the way he made her feel special, their closeness—she couldn't deny it—those were the things she didn't trust. Drew was seeing her good side. What would happen when he saw the bad side? The one who unintentionally hurt kids in her care?

He'd be done with her. He wouldn't look at her like she was special anymore. That's why she couldn't succumb to the lure of him. He probably didn't know he was alluring.

Families and older couples filed into the pews around her. She flipped through her bulletin but couldn't focus. Which brought her thoughts back to Treyvon.

Fifteen. So young. And he'd tried hard to stay out of the gang life before his grandmother fell ill. Lauren had studied the reports from school. He'd gotten good grades. Was never tardy. Had excellent attendance.

Yet he was in juvenile detention until he turned eighteen.

And then what?

Where would he go? What would he do? Who was counseling him? How had Jay's death affected him? She didn't want to think about these things, but there they were. Whispering. Shouting.

He'd made a terrible mistake, but didn't he deserve a chance at a good life?

Would he have that chance?

Her chest tightened at his reality. No support system. No money. Nowhere to go after his sentence was served.

Organ music began to play, and her parents shuffled in beside her.

"You're here." Mom beamed, sitting next to her. "I'm so glad you came."

Dad sat next to Mom and leaned over to wink. "Good to see you, sweetheart."

"How's Wyatt been?" Mom whispered. "When you brought him over the other night, my heart broke at how pale he was. Dad and I want to help in any way we can. Maybe we could all go to a water park or take the boat out or something. Get his mind on fun stuff again."

"Thanks, Mom. That's a good idea. I stayed with him Friday. He's still not himself. He barely talked and seemed withdrawn." Lauren frowned. He wasn't just withdrawn. He'd been spending a lot of time by himself, and it bothered her.

Mom patted her hand. "That's understandable. The poor dear."

"Tell him I've got the telescope out," Dad said. "He can come over and look at the stars any night he wants."

"He'll like that. You busy tomorrow night?"

"We're not busy, but it's supposed to be cloudy. He wouldn't be able to see much."

"We'll figure out another time later this week."

The pastor opened the service, and Lauren sank back, ready to worship. The opening hymn was a favorite of hers.

"Have you ever had someone say the exact thing you needed to hear?" The pastor stood at the pulpit. "Maybe you were nervous about a child or a performance review, and, randomly, you ran into someone who unwittingly calmed your fears with their words. In *First Thessalonians*, chapter five, we're told to 'encourage each other and build each other up, just as in fact you are doing.'"

Is that why Treyvon had been on her mind? She'd thought not being his caseworker was the end of her season with him. But maybe she'd been wrong. Could she help him, not as a social worker but as a friend?

Did she even want to?

The service continued, and the sense of not having closure about Treyvon grew. Was it too late to make an impact on his life?

She clutched her hands together until the knuckles turned white. Would he want to hear from her? How would she go about it? It wasn't like she could show up at the detention center and demand he speak to her. She didn't want to demand anything. She wanted...

She wanted his forgiveness.

His forgiveness?

She loosened the grip on her hands. She'd told herself Treyvon was to blame for Jay's death, but she'd blamed herself, too. And she'd blamed God for letting it happen. And Jay for sneaking out late at night in a dangerous neighborhood. And his mother for being a drug addict. And his grandmother for dying.

Lord, I've blamed everyone except the garbageman, and I could probably find a way to blame him, too. None of them shot Jay, though. I want to let go of this.

The strains of another hymn flowed, and she grabbed the hymnal to join in. She didn't let her thoughts wander the remainder of the service.

Soon she followed her parents out of the church to join everyone on the lawn. Her breathing hitched when she caught sight of the back of Drew's dark head. She craned her neck—yep, Wyatt was with him. She hadn't realized they attended her church.

"Oh, there are Drew and Wyatt. Let's go say hi." Mom bustled in their direction.

"Lauren and I were just talking about you," Dad said, addressing Wyatt. "You know the telescope I mentioned? I found it in the shed and set it up. Lauren will bring you around sometime this week if you want to see the moon and stars up closer."

Wyatt's face lit with a smile. "Really? That would be cool."

Lauren met Drew's eyes. Appreciation glittered within.

"Well, I have an idea." Mom tapped her chin with her finger. "Why don't you all come to dinner at our house Wednesday night? Drew, are you working that night?"

"I have Wednesday off." Drew smiled. "We'd love to come over. If it's not too much trouble…"

"No trouble at all. Bill will grill some burgers, and we can have a bonfire. How does that sound, Wyatt?"

Wyatt nodded happily. "And we can look through the telescope then. Lauren, can we go to the library and get books out about constellations?"

She was taken aback by his animation. "Of course. We'll go tomorrow."

"Awesome!"

"Okay, let's plan on seven. See you kids then." Mom took Dad's arm. They waved and headed to the parking lot. Her parents had always gone out of their way to include people, to help others. What would they do in her situation with Treyvon?

If she had to guess, she'd say they would offer an invitation. Like the one they'd just offered to Drew and Wyatt.

Drew raised his eyebrows. "Big plans this afternoon? Wyatt and I are taking the boat out to go fishing. You're welcome to join us."

She smiled and shook her head. "Sorry. Maybe next time. I have something I need to do."

No sense in wasting time. She was writing Treyvon a letter. Today.

She just wanted the kid to know he wasn't alone. He had someone who cared about him. After that, well, it was up to God to work on Treyvon's heart.

"He hasn't stopped poring over those books you got him the other day." Drew gathered the ketchup and mustard and followed Lauren through the sliding door into her parents' house Wednesday night. They'd eaten cheeseburgers and pasta salad on the deck, and Wyatt and Bill were carrying the telescope to a clear area on the lawn. Bill claimed it was the best spot to see the stars. Lauren's mom had gone upstairs to put a load of laundry in the dryer, leaving Drew and Lauren alone to clean up. He didn't mind.

His thoughts about Chase had been troubling him lately. Part of him wanted to discuss them with Lauren, but the other part wasn't so sure.

"Wyatt? Poring over a book?" Juggling the pasta salad and an empty platter in her hands, she glanced back over her shoulder and grinned. "Better take a picture of that."

"Already did." He opened the refrigerator and found room on the shelves for the condiments. Lauren turned on the faucet and squirted dish soap in the sink. The window poured light on her features. *Beautiful.* He leaned against the counter, crossing one ankle over the other, and watched her slide plates into the soapy water.

"Well, his interest in the solar system has taken his mind off photographers." Lauren washed and rinsed the dishes and set them on the dish rack. Drew crossed over to help.

"I didn't tell him, but one of the guys at work said his sister—she works at Quick Cuts—was trimming a guy's hair, and he asked about Chase McGill and if it was true his son lived here. She didn't reveal anything to the guy, but she wanted me to know."

Lauren rinsed another dish, her bouncy demeanor sober. "I don't understand people like that. Doesn't he see what he's doing?"

"Those reporters consider celebrities fair game." Drew took the dish from her hand, their fingers touching.

"Fine. Celebrities choose their career. But their kids?" With her lips drawn together, she shook her head. "Unbelievable."

"I know. Eventually they'll realize there's no story here and leave him alone."

"They'd better."

"And we'll do everything we can to make them feel unwelcome if they do show up." Drew dried the silverware. For the past week, his coworkers had treated him like one of them. They'd been concerned about Wyatt, and they'd gone out of their way to help him protect the kid. What a change from when he'd started. "In the meantime, I was hoping Wyatt's interest in the solar system would have gotten him off this football obsession, but it hasn't."

Lauren finished the few dishes and wiped the counter. "I take it Wyatt hasn't given up on his football dreams?"

"No. He keeps bringing it up. Whining about it. Getting mad. I don't know what to do."

She folded the dishcloth over the sink. "Come on—let's talk out on the deck."

They went back outside and sat on lawn chairs. In the distance Wyatt bent to adjust the telescope and Bill crouched next to him. The green lawn spread out for almost an acre before disappearing into a tree line. What a perfect summer night. Not too hot. No mosquitoes. The sun still shining for another hour at least.

"So what did you mean about not knowing what to do? I thought you were respecting Chase's wishes." Lauren extended her legs on the chair.

Drew mimicked her, stretching his legs out on the cushion. Before moving to Lake Endwell, he'd followed Chase's instructions to the letter. But something about the move had changed him—was still changing him—and he didn't know what to do about it.

"I was. I am." He rubbed his hand over his cheek. "But lately I've been thinking Chase is wrong. I get he thinks he's protecting him, but shouldn't Wyatt have some say in his life?"

And shouldn't I?

"Do you think football will be good for him?" Lauren asked.

"I don't know. But good or bad, we learn from experience. He's just going to resent me and nurture some unrealistic fantasy about football if I don't let him try it."

"So you're worried about him resenting you?"

That's why he liked talking to her. She figured out the heart of what he was saying before he even did.

"Kind of."

"He probably will at times no matter what you do. You're his parent now. Kids don't like being disciplined." She smiled. "He'll appreciate it when he's older."

"And in the meantime he'll hate me."

Lauren swung her legs over and faced him. "This football thing. Is it about not wanting Wyatt mad at you or you wanting what's best for him?"

He swatted a fly away from his shorts. He could handle Wyatt being mad at him. The kid hadn't wanted to move here, and they'd worked through it. Homework? Same thing. This was different.

"I want what's best for him."

Lauren nodded. "I know you do."

"I just don't get why I can't make some of these decisions. I'm the one raising him for the next several years. Shouldn't I have some say?" As soon as the words were out of his mouth, he wanted to take them back. Who was he to question Chase's desires for Wyatt? It wasn't as if Drew had kids or any parenting experience. And Chase was a great dad.

"Have you talked to Chase about it?"

"Yeah, and he's as stubborn as Wyatt. I'm getting nowhere with either of them."

"Puts you in a tough spot."

It sure did. He didn't like having people mad at him. Part of him had been trying to avoid disappointing anyone ever since his college fiasco.

"Technically you're Wyatt's guardian. You can override Chase about this."

"But should I?"

"I don't know. Will it kill Wyatt not to play football? Plenty of kids get through life fine without it."

"And plenty of kids get through life fine *with* it."

"Sounds like you've made your mind up."

He sighed. "Not really."

"Have you prayed about it?"

"No." Why hadn't he prayed about it? His prayers tended to revolve around keeping Wyatt safe and helping people he loved. He rarely prayed for himself.

Why didn't he pray for himself?

Because I don't deserve anything more than I already have.

Lauren's mom slid the patio door open. "Lauren, Drew? Would you mind driving to the Bradley Farm and getting some firewood? I'll have Bill start a bonfire later. Oh, and pick up graham crackers, marshmallows and Hershey's bars. I'm hungry for s'mores."

"Okay, Mom."

Drew stood and offered his hand to Lauren. She placed her soft hand in his, and he hauled her to her feet. He caught his breath at her nearness. Tanned face, sun-kissed hair and pink lips—tempting. Too tempting.

Her eyes flickered from his eyes to his mouth, and her cheeks flushed.

Maybe she felt it, too. He stood taller, his pulse racing. How could he fight this attraction when she looked at him that way?

I don't deserve—

Wait.

Why not?

Why didn't he deserve her? Why was he so sure he was bad for her?

Because if he started believing he deserved her, he'd give his whole heart away. And if she didn't want it, it would be worse than getting kicked out of college. And just like then, he'd have no one to blame but himself.

Lauren climbed out of Drew's truck at the farm outside town. They'd enjoyed an easy silence driving here with the windows down. It had given her time to think. About Drew's situation and how pleased she was he confided in her. She hadn't told anyone about writing Treyvon. She wasn't sure why. She'd considered telling her parents and Megan, but what if they thought it was a dumb move? Or said something she didn't want to hear? But Drew...she could tell him. He never seemed to think less of her when she confessed her secrets. Would he now?

Her sandals flapped against the gravel drive, and Drew strolled by her side as they approached a stand full of logs. A small box with a padlock and a slot for cash was attached to the side.

"One bundle or two?" Drew stopped, legs wide, before the logs stacked into dividers. Each section was considered a bundle. His muscles strained under his faded navy T-shirt, and she let out a tiny sigh at all the male strength standing in front of her. How had Megan described him? *Tall, built and studly. Yep.* That about summed it up.

"Two." She yanked a log out and carried it in both arms back to his truck.

"You don't have to do that. I can carry them." He jogged to catch up with her, motioning to take the log out of her arms.

"I've carried them a hundred times with my dad." She kept moving until she reached the bed of the truck, dropping it in with a thunk. "It's no big deal."

He took her hand. Her heartbeat hammered. What was he doing? Gently, he flipped her hand over and trailed his finger up her forearm. She shivered.

"The wood scratched you." His fingers lingered on the tender skin. And the look in his eyes? Her heart was going to beat right out of her chest. This was the second time in less than an hour she'd thought about kissing him.

Kissing him? No way. Not smart.

"It's just a little mark. No big deal." She dropped her arms by her side. Turning, she headed back to the stand. "Did I tell you I finally applied for the counselor position at the high school?"

"That's great." His smile grew. "You still thinking about being the cheerleading coach, too?"

"I sure am." She hauled another log into her arms. He did the same. "I know I can handle being a cheer coach. And I'm feeling a little better about the counselor position. I talked with Megan about it and researched the job a bit. I know I'd be dealing with teenagers with emotional problems, but I'd also be interacting with a lot of teens who don't have those problems. From what I can tell, I'd be helping upperclassmen with college decisions and adjusting students' schedules. I think I can handle that."

"I know you can handle it." He hoisted three logs as easily as if they were rolled-up newspapers.

"Well, I still have to be interviewed. It's not a sure thing." She dropped her log in the back of the truck. "Can I tell you something?"

"Of course."

"Remember how I told you about the boys in Chicago?"

"How could I forget?" He stacked the wood in the truck bed, and they went back to the stand for another round.

"I've been thinking about Treyvon a lot."

"You still mad at him?"

"No. I'm...well, I'm worried about him. I tried to

put him out of my mind, but he kept coming back. I wrote him a letter."

Drew grabbed three more logs but didn't say anything.

"I got to thinking about a few years from now. What will happen to him? He'll be out of juvenile detention, but where's he going to go? Back to his mom? Back to the gang? His brother's dead, his grandmother's dead and he has nothing to fall back on."

Drew's jaw clenched. He took big strides to the truck. She fought to keep up with him. After he stacked the remaining logs, he wiped his forehead with the back of his hand. "So what did you put in the letter?"

She brushed her hands on her shorts. "I apologized. For not getting him and Jay out of the house sooner. For not finding them a safe environment. I told him I blamed myself for failing him and Jay, and I told him about my childhood. I checked with the detention center. They won't let him call me, but he can write. I sent writing supplies and stamps. Told him to write back if he wanted to."

"That's all?" They stood behind the truck. He cocked his head to the side.

"Isn't it enough?"

"For a minute there I thought you were going to say you invited him to live with you when he gets out."

She hadn't thought about it. "And if I had?"

"I'd worry." He stepped closer to her.

"Yeah?" Her pulse took off in a sprint.

"Because he might have gone into juvie a scared kid, but he could come out a hardened man."

"I don't know what will happen to him, but I want him to know I care. I hope he writes me." She lowered her gaze to the ground.

Drew brushed the back of his hand down her hair. The touch startled her, and she stared into his eyes. Got lost in their rich brown depths.

He leaned in, his lips grazing hers. And she met him, pressing hers to his.

The kiss was the definition of Drew. Strong yet gentle. Confident and generous. All man. All Drew.

She put her palms against his chest, and without thought, slid them up around the back of his neck, getting closer to him, kissing him back. Instantly, his hands wrapped around her lower back, holding her tightly.

She was lost in a sea of sensation. The scent of his cologne, the warmth of his skin, the taste of his lips, the sound of her heartbeat thudding in her ears.

They pulled away at the same time, remaining in each other's arms.

"We shouldn't—" Lauren turned her head to the side. Kissing him, standing in his embrace felt so good. But her head shouted, *No, no, it's all wrong! Protect yourself!*

He cleared his throat. "Uh, yeah. Complicates things too much."

Her heart dropped to the gravel under her sandals. The words were right. So why did they sound so wrong? She was falling for him. And she had no idea how to make it stop.

Drew clutched a coffee mug and watched the sun rise over the lake the next morning. He stood on the dock in front of his cottage. Pink-and-purple clouds spread into blue. Steam wreathed above his mug, reminding him to enjoy his coffee while it was hot. Speaking of heat... What had possessed him to kiss Lauren yesterday? When she'd said they shouldn't, he'd snapped back to reality. Of course they shouldn't. They were in a complicated relationship, and Wyatt was at the center. What would it do to the kid if he and Lauren started dating only to break up? Wyatt needed stability. And Drew needed...

His mind flashed to her soft lips. How magnificent she felt in his arms. He'd wanted to keep her there forever. To hold. To protect. To love.

Love. He'd never really been in love. There were a few times in his past when he'd thought he'd been, but back then the only one he'd loved was himself.

Could he say the grown him was any different?

Yes.

Where had that yes come from?

He took a tentative drink of coffee. Hot but not scorching.

I've changed. Lauren had helped him see it. He could almost believe he was worthy of loving her.

Almost.

She'd surprised him yesterday when she'd talked about writing Treyvon. He'd never thought about the kid's future. It wouldn't occur to him.

But caring was in her DNA.

He hoped the kid wouldn't disappoint her.

God, please don't let this kid be another negative in her life. Help her see her life matters. Show her she didn't fail anyone. I'm not asking for me—

He frowned. Did he always end his prayers with "I'm not asking for me"?

Yes, his prayers usually had a stipulation he wasn't praying for himself.

Okay, Lord, I am asking for me. What in the world do I do about Lauren? I care about her. A lot. It's veering toward love, and I know that's not wise. But what am I supposed to do? I'm drawn to her. I can tell her things I don't tell anyone else. And I want to spend time with her. When we're together, I feel right. Good. At peace.

He gazed out over the lake glistening under the rising sun. Calm. If he wanted to be at peace, he could feel it here. Without Lauren.

He didn't want to mess up her life. She'd said they shouldn't, and he had agreed. Better to preserve their friendship than to throw it away for a risky shot at more.

Chapter Ten

Where had Wyatt gone?

Lauren stretched her neck to see beyond the massive playground to the swings and tennis courts nearby. She and Drew had resumed their nonkissing relationship. They hadn't been talking as much, either, but it was for the best. Had it only been a week since he kissed her? She'd never be able to buy firewood from that farm again without remembering his lips pressed against hers.

Principal Gilbert had called two days ago to set up a phone interview next week about the counseling position. Apparently the school had a process, starting with a phone interview. Lauren had also signed up for a cheerleading certification course. The certification manual had arrived, so while Wyatt had been running around the play structure with a pack of boys his age, she'd studied it to prepare for the timed exam.

But now it was getting late. She needed to find Wyatt and stop at the grocery store for a few dinner items. She ambled around the perimeter of the large park. Children of all ages laughed and chased one another across the wooden bridges and slides. But she didn't see Wyatt or his friends.

An uneasy feeling came over her, but she shushed it. No need to panic. He had probably run to the bathroom without telling her.

Wyatt still wasn't talking to her as much lately. Between the prison visit and the photographer incident, she'd figured he was working through complicated issues and needed some space. He didn't have a cell phone, but he did have an iPod with an app to text his friends. Had she been wrong to let him have his space?

She broke into a light jog, looking for his light brown hair and skinny legs and black basketball shorts. Around the corner, she spotted him and the other boys lined up at the water fountain.

Relief made her stand still a moment. Of course he was there. Just getting a drink with his friends the way any ten-year-old would.

She waved to him. "Wyatt, we need to leave."

He held a finger up. The boys gathered closer to him, discussing something. She narrowed her eyes. It was so hard to know if they were good kids or schemers.

Wyatt trudged her way, flushed but not smiling.

"Did you have fun?"

"Yeah."

"Don't sound so excited." She strode across the lawn to the parking lot. He didn't crack a smile or say a word. They buckled up and drove to Lake Endwell Grocery.

"You grab a cart, while I try to remember what I need." Lauren gestured to the carts. She needed to know more about those kids he was hanging around, but his quiet, closed-off wall wasn't giving her much to work with. Maybe they could do something fun tonight, and she could figure out how to approach him later. Wyatt pushed a cart, and they weaved through the produce aisle. "So what do you want to do after dinner? We can fish on the end of the dock, play some beach volleyball or rent a movie."

He shrugged, turning away.

Okay, then. She tossed a prebagged salad mix into the cart and moved to the meat department. After selecting a package of chicken breasts and a bottle of Italian dressing, they stopped at the ice-cream aisle.

"Moose Tracks or Oreo Explosion." She pointed to the glass door.

Wyatt sighed. "Oreo Explosion, I guess."

She added a carton to the other items and continued to the checkout lanes. Wyatt walked ahead of her to the magazines, pulled one off the shelf and held it in both hands, not moving.

The headline read, "My Life in Jail." She didn't recognize the man on the cover, but the name hit her like a bucket of ice water. Chase McGill.

Wyatt dropped the magazine and covered his face with his hands. She gathered him to her, but every muscle in his little body had tensed. A tap on the arm might shatter him. Her heart filled with indignation and pity. How much more could this kid take?

"Come on—let's go outside." Lauren left the cart and looked at the checkout girl. "I'm sorry. We have an emergency. I can't buy these now."

"Did you want us to hold them?"

Lauren shook her head and hustled Wyatt out the door to her car. Her apartment was nearby, and she didn't debate it—just drove to her place, helped him up the steps and made him stretch out on the couch. Then she wet a washcloth and set it on his forehead. She sat on the other end of the couch, unlaced his sneakers and put his feet in her lap.

He hadn't said a word. Wasn't crying. He looked devastated.

Zingo strutted to the couch and hopped right onto Wyatt's stomach.

"No, Zingo. Now's not a good time." But the cat sat on Wyatt's chest, staring at his face. Wyatt reached up to pet him, and the kitty got comfortable, folded his legs and started purring.

"Can I get you anything? Do you want to talk?"

Wyatt didn't move, didn't respond. Just kept stroking Zingo's fur.

Lauren didn't know what to do. How did moms handle things like this? Well, most moms didn't have to worry about their son seeing a big photograph of his father on a magazine with a caption about life in jail. And it wasn't as if Lauren was Wyatt's mom. He didn't have one. She'd have to do for now.

Of all the selfish things to do, why had Chase chosen this? Didn't he realize how difficult life was for Wyatt? Shouldn't he know Wyatt wouldn't want everyone reading about his dad's life in jail?

What should she say? What did Wyatt need?

Lord, I don't know what to do. What do I do?

She slipped into her bedroom, shut the door and leaned against it, blowing out a breath. As the air released, she curled her hands into fists. Anger wouldn't help this situation. She massaged the back of her neck with both hands. No wonder the photographer had just happened to show up when he did. Probably knew the article was coming out and wanted to capitalize on it by selling pics to the tabloids. *Scumbag.*

She cracked the door open to peek out at Wyatt. His

hands rested on Zingo, who'd fallen asleep. She tiptoed out there. Wyatt's eyes were closed, too. Probably exhausted from the playground and the shock.

Padding to the kitchen, she picked up her phone and debated her first move. Drew needed to know. She'd better call him. And she'd text Megan to pick her up a copy of the magazine. It would be better for Wyatt if they knew exactly what was in the article.

She cringed as it hit her that his friends could read it. Would they tease him? Bully him? Stop hanging out with him? She peeked at Wyatt's sweet face, her heart cracking. None of this had been easy on him, and it wouldn't get any easier if Chase didn't start putting his son first.

She returned to her bedroom, shutting the door behind her. She pressed Drew's number. If Chase were here, she'd give him a piece of her mind. But he wasn't. As usual, Drew would be left picking up the pieces of Chase's mistakes. Lauren would do anything necessary to help Drew and to protect Wyatt from his father's careless decisions.

Even if each passing day left her heart unguarded and more vulnerable where Drew was concerned.

Wyatt didn't have anyone but Drew and her. She'd be there for both of them, for as long as it took. At some point they wouldn't need her anymore, and she'd have to move on without them. But for now she was part of their lives. And she was going to let Drew know exactly what she thought of Chase's actions.

Drew sprayed the side of the fire truck one final time. He liked this part of the job, cleaning the equipment, making sure it was ready for the next call. The warm summer sun bounced off the stream of water, causing a miniature rainbow to appear. He grinned. A little reminder God was watching.

His cell phone buzzed. He turned off the hose and wiped his hands on a towel before answering. "Drew here."

"We have a problem."

Dread knotted his stomach at Lauren's tone. What could this be about? "What's going on?"

"Well, it seems your best friend thought it would be wise to have *People* magazine interview him. He obviously had no consideration for Wyatt or his feelings. I can't believe Wyatt had to see his dad's face on the cover with the headline, 'My Life in Jail.' Doesn't he have any clue how this affects his son?"

He blinked. Fury poured out of her words, but it took a moment before their impact hit him.

The *People* interview. He smacked his forehead. He'd forgotten...hadn't really given it much thought. When Chase wanted to do something, he did it. Drew never interfered. Figured he was a grown man and could make his own decisions.

"Chase told me he was doing it." Drew used his free hand to pick up the rags next to the truck.

"What?" That was a loaded word if he'd ever heard one. He'd be smart to tread carefully with Lauren in an angry mood. She continued, "And you didn't talk him out of it?"

Looking back, he should have talked him out of it. He hadn't thought it was a big deal. Hadn't considered how it would affect Wyatt.

Why hadn't it occurred to him Wyatt would be hurt?

Because he wasn't like Lauren, who instantly recognized how events would affect others. He was always two steps behind in the consideration department, and Wyatt always seemed to be the one who paid for it.

"You're right," Drew said, throwing the rags into an empty bucket with more force than necessary. "I should have talked him out of it. I didn't think. It's my fault." And now he'd have to do damage control to a kid who'd had enough damage for a lifetime.

"Are you kidding me?" Her voice rose to new decibel levels. "Don't you dare take the blame for this. I know Chase is your friend, but come on. You weren't the one who agreed to the interview. He did. He needs to take responsibility for this. For going after that guy. For ending up in jail. For all of it!"

He held the phone an inch from his ear. Wow, she was really worked up. "Calm down—"

"Don't tell me to calm down."

"Okay." He pinched the bridge of his nose. "What do I do? I can't come over right now. I'm on duty. Do you want to bring Wyatt over here? I can talk to him. If you give me an hour, I should be able to find a replacement."

"Don't bother." Her tone softened. "He's resting. I asked Megan to buy me a copy of the magazine so we can read it and figure out the best way forward. If you want to do something, call Chase and tell him he just ruined his son's life all over again."

"Hey now. It's not like he set out to hurt Wyatt."

"I don't care what he set out to do. The result's the same."

He clutched the phone, fantasizing about throwing it a hundred yards downfield, getting the perfect spiral on it while he was at it. Man, he hated this helpless feeling.

"What's done is done," he said. "How do we move forward?"

"Megan is renting movies and bringing a pizza over

to my apartment. We're going to distract Wyatt tonight. When you get home in the morning, we'll figure out our next move. Come to my apartment when your shift ends."

"I can try to get someone to cover for me tonight."

"No. We can handle him. We'll talk in the morning." She sounded as if she was going to hang up.

"Wait, Lauren?"

"What?"

"What are you going to say to him tonight?" He didn't want her bad-mouthing Chase in front of Wyatt, but how could he ask her not to? This situation grew more complicated each second.

"I don't know."

"I know you're upset with Chase, but can I ask you not to talk bad about him?"

"I'm not stupid, Drew. Chase is Wyatt's dad. Of course I'm not going to trash-talk him. I *will* be discussing choices and how they affect the ones close to us, though. Wyatt has every right to be upset with his dad."

"Fair enough."

"I'll call if anything comes up."

The phone went dead, and with a heavy step, he put the rest of the cleaning supplies away. His heart was torn. Should he ignore Lauren's advice and call someone in for him?

She could handle it. Megan could, too. Wyatt had never had a real mother figure in his life. It would probably do the kid good to have two women fussing over him. Besides, he had a feeling if he showed up, he'd get a verbal lashing he would *not* enjoy. He was in the doghouse, and he deserved it.

After he'd parked the truck back in the garage, he went up to the living quarters and sank into a couch.

Why hadn't he thought about Wyatt when Chase mentioned the interview? Did he have to be hit over the head with a two-by-four to realize the article would be a bad move for Wyatt? He should have asked Chase not to do it.

Don't you dare take the blame for this.

Drew covered his face with his hands.

Lauren was right. He'd been picking up the pieces left from Chase's mistakes for too long. In a few months, it would be a year since Missy had died. The previous ten months unfolded in Drew's memory, and anger shot through his veins. He'd nipped this rage in the bud countless times since Chase was arrested, but right now he had no energy left to fight it.

When Chase drove off to confront Len, Chase hadn't thought about anyone but himself. And he continued to make decisions based solely on his emotions. His needs.

Oh, you wanted to be the big guy about Missy. You didn't care about her when she lived in Chicago and was spiraling out of control from the drugs. You never married her, but you had to go off and avenge her death, huh? What about us? What about me? I miss you. You're my best friend. And Wyatt? You are everything to him, and I'm a sloppy substitute. If it wasn't for Lauren, who knows what kind of emotional shape Wyatt would be in right now?

And this article—this stupid article. You feel guilty, do you, buddy? So you want the media and all your fans to see you've learned your lesson? Well, what about Wyatt? Lauren is right. What kid wants his friends to see his dad's face on the cover of a magazine with that headline?

Drew jumped to his feet and paced the room. Wanted to punch the wall.

He strode to the weight room and pummeled the punching bag until his energy drained.

"What crawled down your shorts? That bag isn't the enemy, you know." Tony stood in the doorway, his arms crossed over his chest.

Drew wiped the sweat from his forehead. "Everything."

"Drama queen." He crossed the room and gestured for Drew to follow him into the living area. "What's really going on?"

"Lauren just called—"

"Are you two dating or what?"

"Forget it." Drew glared.

Tony threw his hands up in defense. "What? You two have *couple* written all over you, but whatever. Live in denial, brother. Continue."

Drew didn't have the energy to contemplate Tony's words. "Chase is on the cover of *People* magazine."

"And you're jealous?"

"Are you kidding me? Of course not." Drew stood up so quickly his head spun. "I'm thinking about Wyatt. How would you like it if your dad was on the cover of a national magazine with a headline about being in jail?"

"Oh. That kind of cover." Tony grimaced, waving him to sit back down. "Hey, I know I give you a hard time, but I give you a lot of credit for moving back and taking care of Wyatt. It can't be easy."

"Wyatt is easy. Even if he was the worst kid in the world, he'd be easy. I love him. And, well, Chase is my best friend."

"But you're mad at him."

Drew swallowed. *Yeah.* He was. "I shouldn't be."

Tony scoffed. "Why not? I'd be mad. You went

from single to legal guardian overnight. If it was me, I wouldn't want to move and leave my fire station."

"I didn't want to move. They were my brothers."

"You've got new brothers."

Drew met Tony's eyes and nodded. "I appreciate it, man."

"When you started, I was sure you were going to be the superstar quarterback who left town after high school. You've changed. You've got a lot to complain about, but you never do. The guys look up to you. I was wrong about you."

He didn't know how to respond. He'd never expected to hear those words from Tony, of all people.

"I appreciate it, Tony. But I don't have anything to complain about. I'm doing what I love with good people. I've been blessed."

"That's where we differ. I'd complain." Tony grinned. "So what's the deal with you and Lauren?"

"Nothing. She's Wyatt's babysitter."

"You don't look at her like she's just a babysitter."

"Does any guy look at her like she's just a babysitter?"

"Point taken."

Drew rubbed his chin. "She chewed me out. Bigtime."

Tony chuckled. "If she's chewing you out, that's a good sign."

He shook his head. "It's not like that."

"You going to be a bachelor forever? A girl like Lauren Pierce doesn't come around that often. She's single, but for how long? You should make your move."

"I've got enough to think about without dealing with a relationship."

"Have it your way, but don't come crying to me when she starts dating someone else."

Was Tony trying to give him a stroke? Drew wanted to date her. But...if she wasn't helping with Wyatt, he'd be lost. He couldn't jeopardize their working relationship to explore a personal one. And today had driven home what he'd known all along: Lauren would never be interested in someone as selfish as him. She put other people's needs before her own. He didn't even know what other people's needs were.

If he couldn't rely on her to babysit Wyatt, he'd be back to where he started. And Wyatt would be the casualty. They both needed her. He'd lock up his attraction to Lauren and bury the key.

"How is he?"

"Sleeping." Lauren followed Drew into her living room the next morning. He held a take-out tray with three cups in one hand and a paper bakery bag in the other. She'd woken this morning calm. Life was too short to cling to anger, even if it was justified. Ultimately, her hot emotions wouldn't help Wyatt. A cooler head would.

After Wyatt woke from his nap yesterday, she and Megan had plied him with pizza and silly movies until it had grown late. They'd waited until he was asleep before reading the magazine article. She had to hand it to Chase; he sounded contrite in it.

"Where is he sleeping?" Drew tossed the bag on the table and set the drink tray down.

"He's in my office. I set up my sleeper sofa for him."

"Thank you." He put the tray down and turned to her. "I feel like such a jerk."

She craved his embrace. Hadn't realized how draining the night had been, how much she yearned for his physical support right now. But just because they acted as Wyatt's parents didn't make them anything more than a guardian and a babysitter. She had no right to step into the role of parent. And she had no right to step into Drew's arms and ask him to hold her, either. So she didn't.

"You're not a jerk. We'll handle this, and Wyatt will, too. It's probably not going to be easy for him, though. You know how awful some kids can be. They smell weakness and pounce."

"Yeah, I do. I was one of those kids. You should know." The muscle in his cheek jumped.

"And you changed." She pressed her palm to his face, meeting his eyes. "I forgave you a long time ago. Isn't it time to let it go?"

"If you say so." He passed her a coffee. "Full of cream and sugar. Just the way you like it."

He remembered how she liked her coffee? Her throat tightened. She'd been taking care of herself for years. She'd forgotten what it was like to have someone care enough to remember the little details.

She'd closed herself off for a long time. Hadn't dated. Had devoted all her energy to her job. But maybe she'd been wrong. Maybe having someone who knew the little details—someone who cared—wasn't a bad thing. Maybe this closeness—this taking care of Wyatt's needs together—was what she needed, even if it scared her.

She was getting tired of living life on her own.

Drew sat at the table and opened the bag, sliding a doughnut her way. She sat across from him.

His cheeks puffed out as he exhaled. "Before we get into this, I think you'd better know there's a chance more reporters and photographers will show up here. Articles tend to trigger something in them. The tabloids, especially. When Chase was on trial, every time an article was published, a bunch of photographers would try to get Wyatt's picture." He took a big bite of his doughnut, and when he'd finished chewing, he sipped his coffee.

Zingo trotted up to Drew and jumped on his lap. Drew stared wide-eyed at Lauren as if to say, "What do I do about this?"

"Relax. We've been through this already. It's a cat, not a bomb."

"Sure," he mumbled, petting Zingo. "So what's the plan?"

"Have you seen the article yet?"

"No."

She went to her room, found the magazine and brought it back to him.

He flipped to the article. She watched him as he read it. His eyebrows dipped; then he grunted, and the final paragraph seemed to hit him. He appeared reflective.

"I didn't realize I was mad at him until last night," Drew said softly. "I've rationalized his behavior with excuses, but I haven't admitted how angry I am that he went after Len and landed in jail."

Lauren nodded, not sure what to say. This was a huge step for him. She thought back on all the times Drew blamed himself for Chase's decisions. He'd probably never realized he had a right to be mad.

"I miss him," Drew said softly. "I miss my best friend."

"I know. And you don't have to stay mad at him." She covered his hand with hers. "What do you think of the article?"

"I think his intentions were good. I think it accurately reflects his sincere regret at taking the law into his hands and messing up his life. But I'm tired of him doing things like this without considering the effects on Wyatt. And, honestly, Lauren, if you weren't here, I think Wyatt would be a mess. It hadn't occurred to me the article would affect him. You get him in a way I don't."

He thought too highly of her. She had no idea what she was doing, and Wyatt could end up a mess in her care. She'd made bad decisions before. This job—trying to anticipate Wyatt's needs—was hard. But she wanted to do it. If she could just be sure she wouldn't fail him…

She shook her head. "He wouldn't be a mess. You're exactly what he needs. As far as the article, I agree. I think Chase had good intentions, too." She sipped her coffee and tore off a small bite of a doughnut. "I think we should let Wyatt read it."

"Okay. I have a feeling his friends are going to have a lot to say about it, too. He might lose a few of them."

The food soured in her stomach. "I know."

They sat in silence, sipping coffee. Wyatt shuffled to the table. He rubbed his eyes and yawned. His hair stuck up in back. As soon as he saw Drew, he fell into his arms.

"Hey, buddy. How'd you sleep?"

"Good. Zingo slept with me. He's soft."

Drew kept his arm around Wyatt's shoulders. "I heard about the magazine."

"Oh." Wyatt dropped onto the chair next to him.

"Here, I bought you a hot chocolate. There's a doughnut with chocolate frosting and sprinkles in there, too."

Wyatt plowed into the pastry but stopped midchew when he noticed the magazine on the table.

"We think you should read it." Lauren slid it his way.

"I don't want to."

"Your friends might read it. It's good for you to know what you're dealing with."

"Why did he have to go and be on the cover?" His pitiful eyes tightened Lauren's chest like a screw. "I hate that he's in jail."

"We all do, buddy." Drew clapped his hand on his shoulder. "But I think Chase wants to let other people learn from his mistakes."

Lauren drank her coffee, trying not to stare at Wyatt as he turned the pages and read. When he finished, he closed the magazine and pushed it away from him.

Drew rapped on the table with his knuckles. "I have a feeling we might see more photographers and reporters over the next couple of weeks. So we're all going to be extra careful."

Wyatt slumped, but he nodded his agreement.

"And if your friends talk about the article, be honest with them." Lauren wiped crumbs from her hands. "You don't have to answer any questions, but you don't have to pretend it didn't happen, either."

"I'm not telling them Dad's in jail."

"They all know."

"Well, I don't want to talk about it to them. I don't want any of this!" He lurched to his feet and ran to the office. Drew followed. Lauren almost did, too, but she sighed, knowing he needed to take care of it. She wasn't Wyatt's mother or guardian. If she was going to adjust to not being Wyatt's babysitter this fall, she needed to remember that.

The trouble was she didn't want to adjust to life without them. She wanted to be there for Wyatt every day. Wanted to rely on Drew in a way she'd never relied on a man.

But how could she?

He thought she was good for Wyatt, but what would happen if he realized she wasn't? If she made a poor judgment call that hurt him? He'd move on to someone else. Someone better.

She was better off alone.

Chapter Eleven

References: check. Phone charged: check. Notebook and pen: check.

Lauren's nerves were twitching like sparks from a bonfire. Her interview with Principal Gilbert was in ten minutes. They'd originally scheduled it for yesterday, but a staff meeting had forced the principal to cancel. Lauren had tried to avoid having it while she watched Wyatt; however, the principal's schedule was full. No other time would work.

"Wyatt?" He'd disappeared into his bedroom after lunch. All day he'd been secretive. Or was it her imagination? Drew told her Wyatt had met up with friends at the park the other day. Had they said something to upset him? Taunted him about the article?

If not, what was bothering him?

She straightened her papers on the kitchen counter for the tenth time. Wasn't his dad being in jail and on the cover of a national magazine enough to bother anyone? Two reporters had nosed around town over the weekend, but the people of Lake Endwell had discouraged their questions and politely suggested they leave Wyatt alone.

After knocking on his bedroom door, she peeked inside. He lay on his bed with his knees up, earbuds in and his thumbs moving overtime on his iPod. She didn't like that device. He spent entirely too much time playing video games and texting other kids. The open window allowed a breeze to ripple through the curtain.

"Hey." She stood in the doorway, arms crossed. "I'm going to be on the phone for about thirty minutes. Do you need anything now?"

He shook his head, not looking up from the small screen.

"Okay, I'll be in the kitchen if you need me. We'll do something when I'm done. We could get the inner tubes out and go swimming. How does that sound?"

He didn't bother responding. Tempted to rip the earbuds out and toss the iPod into the trash, she sighed, closing his door behind her. She missed his sweet nature. Wished the kid who'd been so excited to see the stars from her dad's telescope would come back.

Her phone rang, and she hustled to the kitchen where she'd left everything.

"Lauren, it's Principal Gilbert. Thank you for accommodating my schedule change."

She chatted with the principal about Lake Endwell High and answered questions about her degree and the type of work she'd done in Chicago.

"I'm reassured about your experience with troubled teens. Your supervisor raved about the work you did. Our community, while quiet, isn't immune to modern teen issues. We have our share of students dealing with typical problems, big and small."

"What kind of problems?" Lauren pressed her hand to her stomach.

"Suicide. Depression. Bullying. Drugs. Alcohol. The usual."

The list triggered anxieties she'd set aside for months. "Would you say you have a high percentage of troubled kids?"

"No, I wouldn't. But we do have students facing challenges, and they need an adult who will guide them appropriately. Someone they can trust."

Trust. Could teens trust her? The way Treyvon and Jay had? She still hadn't heard from Treyvon. He must blame her. She would if she were him.

She'd been a fool to think she could handle this job. What if she counseled someone and they ended up committing suicide? Could she have that on her conscience, too? Her gut churned.

"Of course, if a student seems suicidal or is caught with drugs or alcohol, you would advise the parents to seek appropriate help like therapy or a treatment program. The support you'd provide would be limited. As for the cheerleading coach position, Lake Endwell High would be blessed to have you. You're aware of what's involved?"

After taking a shaky breath, Lauren described her experience and mentioned she was in the process of getting certified. Much easier to talk about cheerleading than the other position.

"If you have any questions, please call. I'll be in touch with you soon," Principal Gilbert said. "Thanks again for your time."

She liked the principal but still wasn't sure she could see herself working at the school. Although the principal's assurance she'd be providing limited support helped. Lauren peeked at her watch. They'd talked almost an hour. She'd better check on Wyatt and get the poor kid out of here.

"Wyatt?" She knocked on his door. No answer. *Big surprise.* His earbuds might be permanently glued to his ears at this point. She cracked the door open.

The bedroom looked the same as it had an hour ago, except Wyatt wasn't there. Video games were piled next to the nightstand. A bin of LEGOS sat on the floor. Shorts and a shirt were thrown without thought next to the hamper. The window was open, and his iPod was on his bed. Maybe he'd gone to the backyard while she was on the phone.

She padded on bare feet to the sliding door and stepped onto the deck. The small backyard was fenced, and there was no sign of Wyatt. She went back inside. He could be in the bathroom.

"Wyatt?" She stilled, listening for him. "Wyatt?"

Okay, now she was getting worried. Where was he? She rushed out the front door, hoping he'd slipped out to the dock or something, but she didn't see him there, either.

Where had he gone?

Panic climbed her throat. He could have been kidnapped. Who knew what kind of crazy person had read that magazine article? Had they hatched a plan to hold Wyatt for ransom, knowing Chase was a multimillionaire athlete?

Calm down. Don't rush into worst-case scenarios.

Wouldn't a more likely reason be he'd left on his own?

She ran back inside, shoved her feet into sandals and grabbed her purse. She paused to check his iPod, but she didn't know his pass code. Before she flipped out completely, she'd better cover any ground she could think of.

He could be at the park. Or the ice-cream shop. Or...

He wasn't allowed to go to any of those places by himself. And he'd never wandered off on his own before. She scratched a quick note telling Wyatt to call her on her cell phone if he came back. Fighting down a choking sensation, she got in her car and backed out of the driveway.

She couldn't prevent the fears drilling through her head. She stopped at the park, slamming the door shut behind her. Running through the play structure, she yelled Wyatt's name. Didn't see him or any sign of his friends, either. She went to the men's bathroom, opened the door. "Wyatt? Are you in there?" But no one answered.

He wasn't at the park.

Covering her eyes, she fought for breath. What could she do? Where could she go?

Get it together. You've got to find him.

She drove to the library, the ice-cream shop and finally ended up right back at Drew's cottage. She hunted through each room and the yard one more time before panic consumed her.

She could barely breathe.

There was one thing left to do. She had to call Drew.

"I can't find him. I don't know where he is and I've looked everywhere. The house, yard, park, library, dock—it's like he vanished!"

Drew froze, the skin at the back of his neck prickling as he held the phone. "Slow down. Start from the beginning."

Lauren's breathing sounded choppy. "I told him to get me if he needed anything. That the interview would only be thirty minutes."

"Did you leave him alone at the house?" Drew tried to make sense of what she was saying, but she sounded distraught. If only he was home and could take her in his arms and calm her enough to understand what she was saying…

"No! Of course not. I was on the phone, and I lost track of time."

"I'll text him."

"He left his iPod at home. What if he's been kidnapped? Or was hit by a car? Or he could have wandered into the woods. Oh, no—the lake! Could he have gone swimming? What if he drowned? I'm going out there right now!"

The phone went dead. He dialed her number, but she didn't answer. He fired into action, rushing down the hall to the chief's office.

The chief looked up from his desk. "What's wrong?"

"Lauren just called. She can't find Wyatt. I'm sorry, but I have to leave. I have to go look for him."

"Go." Chief Reynolds frowned, picking up his phone. "I'll get someone to cover for you. Take the rest of the day off and let me know when you find him."

Relief flooded Drew. He nodded. "Thank you."

"Get out of here. I'll make a few calls. Maybe someone has seen him."

Drew raced to his truck and called Lauren's number again. No answer. He texted, Stay put. I'm looking for Wyatt. The chief is calling around. Call me if you find him.

He peeled out of the lot and tried to think where Wyatt would go. Lauren had said she'd gone to the park, but which one? Wyatt could easily ride his bike to three different parks within two miles. Drew gripped the steering wheel and pressed the accelerator.

He searched City Park first. No sign of the kid. Got back in his truck and drove to the big playground where most of Lake Endwell's youth hung out. The sun blasted his face as he strode around the play structure. He shielded his eyes with his hand, but none of the kids even resembled Wyatt.

Fear clutched his chest, but he inhaled and shook his head. *Keep your head on straight. You have plenty of places to look.*

What about Wyatt's friends? Drew had Hunter's parents' contact information. He gave Hunter's mom a quick call, but she hadn't seen Wyatt, and Hunter was camping up north with his grandparents all week.

Drew drove to the other park, but only a few young children were there. He sat in his truck, deciding his next move. What now?

Wyatt wouldn't try to see his dad, would he? The kid knew better. What about trying to get back to Detroit? *Doubtful.* But he couldn't take that possibility off the table yet.

Lauren had mentioned kidnapping. While the reporters and photographers were nuisances, they were hardly kidnappers. But with the magazine article recently published, who knew what kind of wacko might concoct a get-rich-quick idea?

Pressure built in his temples, and he dropped his forehead to his hands on the steering wheel.

God, I need You. Where is Wyatt? Help me find him. Please keep him safe wherever he is.

All Lauren's scenarios roared back. Kidnapping. Hit by a car. Lost in the woods. Drowning…

He pounded the steering wheel. *No.* He wouldn't let any of it happen. He was going to find Wyatt.

His cell phone rang. He hoped it was Lauren. The screen showed Tony Ludlow.

"Yeah."

"Check the football field behind the middle school," Tony said. "A bunch of kids Wyatt's age go over there for informal practices this time of year to get ready for the rec season next month. I don't know if he's there, but it can't hurt to look."

"It's worth a shot." Drew stared at the trees ahead of him. "Thanks, man. I'll go right now."

"Let me know when you find him."

"Will do."

Drew hung up and drove over the speed limit the short distance to Lake Endwell Middle School. He parked and jogged around the building to the back where a baseball diamond and a large field used for football and soccer sprawled. A dozen or so kids in shorts were running around in the distance. He could hear calls of "Blue 52." One threw a football. As he neared, he recognized Wyatt. Relief almost dropped him to his knees. *Thank You, Lord.*

As soon as the gratitude washed over him, fury erupted from his chest.

Wyatt might be all right, but that kid had a lot of explaining to do.

Drew strode, shoulders back, head high, out onto the field. The air had been full of shouting and laughing, but silence landed as the boys saw him. They parted like the Red Sea. Wyatt met Drew's eyes, and Drew recognized the fear in them.

Good. He should be afraid. Very afraid.

He gripped Wyatt's shoulder. "Come on. We're going home."

Wyatt had to jog to keep up with him on the way

back to the parking lot. Drew didn't care. Kept a tight hold on his shoulder until they reached the truck. Wyatt was the first one inside. The windows were down, but the sticky heat remained. Drew knew better than to drive with this much anger boiling inside his body, so he took a moment to get his breathing back to normal.

He faced Wyatt. "Do you have any idea how worried we were?"

"Sorry," he mumbled, his chin dropping to his chest.

"Sorry isn't going to cut it, Wyatt. What were you thinking? You know we've been worried about all the photographers and reporters coming into town. We thought you might have been kidnapped. Lauren's scared out of her mind." He needed to call her. He pointed at Wyatt. "Don't move."

After hopping out of the truck, he walked a short distance away and called her. This time she picked up.

"What? Do you have news? There's no sign of him—"

His heart ached at how upset she sounded. "Lauren, I found him."

"Is he okay?"

"Perfectly fine. For the moment. Tony tipped me off. Some of the kids play football behind the middle school, and that's where I found him."

"The middle school?"

"Don't worry. I'm handling it. The chief gave me the rest of the night off, so why don't you go home and I'll stop by your apartment later."

"I'm sorry," she whispered.

"I am, too." He hung up and texted Tony to let the guys at the station know he'd found Wyatt. He slipped the phone in his pocket and marched back to the truck. Slammed the door behind him.

"Start from the beginning." His jaw felt wired shut it was so tight.

"I didn't think—"

"You got that right. You didn't think. Didn't think about anyone but yourself. Lauren has been frantic with worry. I've been all over town, trying not to picture you lying in a ditch or being held against your will."

Wyatt shrank into himself. "I'm sorry." His tone shifted to a whine.

"Well, I hope you mean it, because you're going to be sorry before the day is over. Now tell me what happened." His words chopped like a knife, and he made no effort to soften them. He'd been too easy on Wyatt and look what had happened.

"Levi texted me that he wanted me to be on his team today."

"And what did you tell him?"

Wyatt glanced over. "I told him I couldn't."

"That's funny. Here you are. What changed?" He waved his hand toward the field.

He shrugged.

"Tell. Me. How. You. Got. Here."

"It wasn't a big deal." His voice rose. "He kept saying it would be fun. Lauren was busy with her interview, so I didn't think you'd care."

Drew clasped his hands so tightly his fingernails almost drew blood. "You didn't think I'd care, did you? What gave you that impression? Your dad doesn't want you playing football."

"He's not here!"

"But I am." Drew jabbed his thumb into his chest. "Don't you think I care about you?"

"Well, yeah, but…"

"But what? Look, Wyatt, I'm sorry your dad is in jail.

You're not the only one who misses him. But it doesn't change facts. He's still your dad, and I'm your fill-in dad until he gets out. You might not like my rules, but you will obey them. Do you understand?"

"Yes, sir," he whispered.

"I love you, and you scared me. You scared Lauren, too. We aren't keeping you from having friends. If you want to spend time with Levi, we'll have him over."

"You won't let me hang out with him," he muttered.

"Is that right?" Drew clenched his jaw. "I don't recall you asking me to."

"That's because you won't let me play football!"

Drew counted to three. His temper had already surged to nuclear levels, and he needed to bring it down. "Let me get this straight. The only way you can hang out with him is if you play football?"

"Pretty much."

"So he doesn't want to ride bikes, go to the beach, get ice cream? He will only hang out with you on the football field?"

Wyatt shrugged again.

"I think you're making excuses. If it's true this kid won't be friends with you unless you're playing football, than he's not a very good friend." Drew started the truck up. "When we get home, you're going to your room. I have a lot to think about, and you *will* be punished. How did you get here, anyhow?"

"I climbed out the window and rode my bike."

"Well, you'd better go get it. I'll put it in the back of the truck." Drew waited for Wyatt to wheel his bike over, and, after putting it in the truck, Drew drove home.

As they passed houses and fields, he thought about his childhood. How he'd yell to his mom he was playing with his friends. She'd yell out, "Be back before dinner." And he would. He'd grown up in a subdivision outside town. He and his buddies would ride around and shoot hoops in one another's driveways. Just like Wyatt, they'd ride over to the football fields and throw the ball around. His mom never cared.

Maybe he'd come down too hard on Wyatt.

But Drew's childhood had taken place in different times. His father hadn't been a celebrity. Plus, Drew had never snuck out.

Drew stole a peek at Wyatt. The kid had that lost look again, the one he'd worn for months before moving here.

Had he been too hard on Wyatt? Not hard enough? Who knew? He needed a crash course in raising a ten-year-old who happened to be the son of an incarcerated football player. He had no idea how to parent this kid.

Had he given him the impression he could do what-ever he wanted? He didn't want Wyatt to become the same entitled jerk he'd been in high school. Or was Wyatt lashing out at his dad's rule? He seemed to be trying to fit in with kids his age. But that didn't mean he could sneak out and play football when it had been forbidden.

Drew drove down Main Street. He'd have to figure out how to deal with Wyatt, but he also needed to check on Lauren. She'd been an emotional wreck on the phone. Drew turned into the parking lot behind her building.

"Don't make me see Lauren now." Wyatt cowered under his seat belt.

"You owe her an apology."

Wyatt looked ready to cry. "I'll tell her I'm sorry, Uncle Drew. But…but please let me do it tomorrow." Tears slipped down his pale cheeks.

Drew almost refused, but he couldn't. Wyatt seemed to be teetering on the same emotional edge as Lauren

had earlier. Maybe it would be better for all of them if
Drew smoothed things out with Lauren before bringing
Wyatt over. With a loud sigh, he nodded. "First thing
tomorrow. But I need to make sure she's okay. She was
very upset earlier."

He didn't trust Wyatt to leave him alone in the truck
right now. If Lauren's parents were home, they might
not mind watching the kid for him while he checked
on her. Unlike Wyatt, he couldn't wait until tomorrow.

Lauren swiped the hair from her eyes and slid another shirt off the hanger. With jerky hands, she folded it
and shoved it into the suitcase on her bed. Zingo found a
seat on top of the jeans she'd stacked inside the suitcase.

She'd messed up. Always messing up. And it had
taken another bad phone call to acknowledge what she'd
known for months.

She wasn't cut out for helping kids.

Not Wyatt.

Not Treyvon.

Not Jay.

And not any of the high school kids, either. She'd
been stupid to even consider it. And Principal Gilbert
would regret it if she hired her.

She'd put herself and her needs first today, and Wyatt
had paid the price. Her throat constricted for the fiftieth
time since discovering Wyatt was missing. Her fault.

All her fault.

It wouldn't happen again.

And what about Drew? He'd depended on her, and
she'd let him down. Visions of him smiling over coffee, eating breakfast together, the way he'd looked at
her before kissing her—he deserved someone better.
Not an imposter like her.

She'd known she was falling for him, but it wasn't until she'd called him to tell him about Wyatt missing that she knew she'd gone and done it.

She'd fallen in love with him.

And she'd broken his trust and not guarded Wyatt.

The fact that Wyatt was okay had made her collapse in the chair and thank the good Lord, but what if he had been kidnapped? Or drowned? Or any other awful thing? She would never have been able to forgive herself.

She had to get out of Drew's life. She loved him too much to disappoint him again. When he'd called her to let her know Wyatt was safe, she'd told him she was sorry. His reply had thrust a knife in her gut. *"I am, too."*

Of course he was. Sorry he hadn't listened to her all those weeks ago when she'd told him point-blank she wasn't the person for the job. She crushed a blouse between her hands. She'd been trying to overcome her failures her entire life. She'd learned at a young age she had to be good. Or else.

Look at what it had gotten her. No stability in her early years, made fun of constantly during high school, head in the clouds with visions of saving people in college and years and years of heartache in Chicago.

Now this.

A knock sounded at her front door. She wadded up the blouse and scurried down the hall. Drew stood in the doorway.

Fall into his arms. Let him hold you. Let him tell you everything will be all right.

She did none of those things. Instead she pivoted and strode back to the bedroom with him at her heels. Carefully folding the blouse, she braced herself for what he was about to tell her.

"What in the world is going on?" He skewered her with his brown eyes.

"What does it look like?"

"It looks like you're leaving."

"Ding, ding. You win the prize."

"Why?"

"I think we both know I can't do this anymore."

His eyes darkened to almost black. He looked like the warrior he was born to be. A rescuer. A leader. A hero.

But heroes saved the good guys, and she couldn't bear to keep up this charade another minute. She'd been trying to be good for almost thirty years. It was time to throw in the towel.

She'd never be good enough for Drew.

Chapter Twelve

Drew took in the half-filled suitcase on the bed, the cat sitting inside it, hangers on the floor and dresser drawers open. The room looked ransacked. She sure was in a hurry to get out of there. Out of his life.

Pain stabbed his heart, and in that instant he knew. He loved her.

He loved this woman who brought sunshine to his days, who'd coaxed Wyatt out of his protective shell, who cared about everyone more than she did herself.

He loved her, and she was leaving.

"Where are you going?" He knew whatever she was about to say was going to make him bleed. His mind sped to the morning his college football coach had called him into the office and told him he'd been cut from the team. It had been the worst day of his life.

Until today.

Didn't Lauren know this would destroy him?

He needed her. Wyatt needed her.

He shouldn't have let himself fall in love with her. She'd always been too good for him. He didn't deserve her, and he knew it. She must have finally realized it, too.

"I don't know where. Away." She set the blouse next to Zingo and returned to the closet.

She didn't know where she was going? Sounded like she was escaping.

Escaping him. He didn't blame her. He'd pushed and pushed her to help him with Wyatt, even after he knew it would be hard on her. Always thinking of himself.

"Wyatt's with your parents," he said, his voice surprisingly calm. "I hope that's okay. I thought I'd better talk to you before bringing him over."

She didn't meet his eyes. "Mom and Dad are good in situations like this."

He took the sweatshirt out of her hands. "Can we talk?"

"What is there to say?"

Was she being serious? His heart was thumping about a thousand beats per minute. "Let's go to the living room. I can't think with you packing."

She nodded, leading the way, sitting on the edge of the couch, ready to spring up at any moment.

She looked fragile. His agitation subsided, replaced with calm. "Lauren, what's going on?"

"I messed up." Her words tumbled out quickly, nervously. She sounded about ready to cry. "The interview took too long, and I knew something was going on with Wyatt. I knew it. Ever since visiting Chase, he's been acting secretive. I should have kept an eye on him. I should have rescheduled the interview for another time. I failed you. I failed him."

"What? That's crazy. This wasn't your fault." Drew moved to sit next to her, putting his arm around her shoulders.

She jerked away, standing. "It is. I can't do this anymore. You're going to have to find another babysitter.

I'm calling the principal and withdrawing my application. I'm not cut out for working with kids."

His heart was already black and blue, and she'd only said a few words. How could he convince her to stay?

"Go back in there and unpack your suitcase. Wyatt is fine. He snuck out and rode his bike to the middle school because…well, I don't entirely know why, but I do know it had nothing to do with you."

She whirled to him, eyes stricken. "It has everything to do with me. I've been trained to look for signs, and all the signs were there, Drew. Sullen, scared, secretive. Spending too much time on that stupid iPod. I knew he was up to something, but I didn't want to believe it. I can't help anyone until I get my head out of the clouds. You think a parent is going to forgive me when I miss the signs their daughter was suicidal? No. It doesn't work that way." She hugged her arms around her waist.

He wanted to cup her face in his hands and make her look in his eyes and tell her he loved her and how much she meant to him. But she was ready to shatter. So he stayed put.

"There is nothing to forgive, Lauren. You give people hope. I don't want you to be anyone but exactly who you are."

"You say that, but you don't know me, Drew. You don't." Her eyes flashed silver. "I've never been who everyone thought I was. I'm the daughter of a drug addict and a murderer."

"You're the daughter of the King. God Himself."

She shook her head as if she didn't want to hear it. "Remember that duffel bag I told you about? What I didn't tell you is that I pulled a knife on a kid to get it back when I was six years old. Six! What six-year-old threatens someone with a knife? That foster home knew enough to get rid of me."

Each word landed like lead in his gut. He could picture her, a beautiful little girl. His entire being revolted at what she'd been through. He closed the distance between them.

"No six-year-old should have to defend her property herself. You should have had a mom and dad to protect you."

"I did. Later." The anguish gripping her face sent waves of pain through his chest. "They made me feel like I was good enough, but I'm not. I'm just not. I'm never going to be." Her shoulders sagged. She looked drained.

Drew gently took her in his arms. He kissed the hair next to her ear and held her, but she didn't hold him back.

"You're too good, Lauren. You want to help everyone. I don't know why you think you're such a failure. You're everything to me."

She stepped back. "Don't say that. I'm not. You can't depend on me. I'll let you down the same way I let everyone down."

"You wouldn't. You don't." How could he break through this crust of guilt encased around her heart? "I told you a while back I'm here for you. No matter what. That hasn't changed. I...I promise." He almost said the words *I love you*, but he couldn't. Not yet.

"I don't want your promise. I want to be alone." The finality in her tone and the tremors in her arms concerned him. He was getting nowhere with her. He didn't want to make it worse.

"I'll let you be alone for now, Lauren, but I keep my promises. Wyatt had a choice today. He chose to do the wrong thing. Those kids you're so upset about in Chicago? They had a choice, too. The older one could have said no to the gang. The younger could have stayed in his house where he belonged."

"I should have—"

He raised his hand to cut her off. "You know what? You have a choice, too. You can give up on all that's good about you, all that you bring to the world to make it better, or you can accept that life stinks sometimes, and you can keep trying. But I can't force you."

"Please go," she whispered.

Did his promise mean nothing to her? Did *he* mean nothing to her?

What had he expected? He'd known he wasn't good enough for her. Told himself over and over he'd get hurt if he let himself fall in love. He'd been living a dream—just like when he'd been on the college football team—and now the dream was over. Except this was worse. Much worse.

He wished he would have taken his own advice when he'd moved back and never let himself fall for Lauren Pierce.

He walked down the hall and left her apartment.

Lauren dropped onto the couch. Everything Drew said swirled, conflicted, collided in her brain. She didn't even know where to begin to make sense of today. The only thing she knew? He was wrong about her.

She couldn't get her head straight in this matchbox of an apartment. It suffocated her. She shoved her feet into athletic shoes, grabbed her keys and phone and ran out the door. When she got to the sidewalk, she didn't think, just jogged in the direction of the lake.

The truth of Drew's words nailed themselves into her soul, but she couldn't quite believe them.

You're the daughter of the King.

The park entrance loomed ahead, and she sped up. Could she outrun his voice? Could she outrun herself?

She sprinted along the trail next to the lake until she hunched over, gasping for breath. Why had she been packing her suitcase? It wasn't as if she had anywhere to go.

I'm still that little girl packing her bag, aren't I?

Exhaustion clawed through her body, and she collapsed on a park bench facing the lake. Seagulls swooped down to the water, calling to each other noisily.

"I am a mess." The words escaped without thought. She turned her head from side to side to see if anyone was around. No one lurked. She sighed in relief. Didn't want to add losing her mind to her list of shortcomings.

She leaned back. The sun warmed her face, and the scent in the air held the tang of the freshwater lake.

God, what am I doing? What do You want me to do?

A squirrel chattered a few yards away. He stood on his hind legs with a nut between his paws. Then he bit into the nut and ran away.

Being a squirrel seemed to be a lot less complicated than being a human.

Why am I making it so complicated?

Drew said they all had choices. She agreed with that. But—

How did she know the right choice? How could she trust herself to make the right decision?

She had a strong urge to go to her parents' house. To talk to her mom.

Had Wyatt and Drew left yet?

She texted her mom. Are you busy? Is Wyatt still there?

Almost instantly her mom replied. Drew picked him up a few minutes ago. Why?

She felt terrible for not seeing Wyatt since Drew found him, but she wasn't ready. She texted Mom back. I'm coming over.

Ten minutes later she found Mom in the kitchen.

"Wyatt upset you today, didn't he?" Mom's loving eyes crashed through the chaos inside her. Lauren drifted into her arms. "It's okay. He's okay. No harm done."

No harm done? She let that one slide and hugged her for a long time. Finally, she broke away.

"Come on," Mom said. "Let's go out to the living room. You can tell me all about it."

She didn't want to tell her all about it, but she followed her, anyway. A vase of daisies brightened the coffee table, and the faint smell of vanilla was in the air from one of her mother's candles. "Mom?"

"Hmm?"

"I'm a mess."

She smiled. "We're all a mess, honey."

"No, I'm truly a mess." Her mom never really got it that some people were more messed up than others. She acted like anything Lauren said or did could be washed clean with one of her dishcloths. "I've always been one."

"That's funny because when I look at you I see a beautiful, caring woman."

I've duped her, too. It's time she saw the real me.

"You see a fake. I've been fooling you and my teachers and everyone for years."

Her mom made a tsking sound. "Lauren, you've never fooled me. You're not a fake."

Would the woman not wake up?

"Look, Mom." Lauren leaned forward. "I was a rotten little girl. Got kicked out of four foster homes. I threatened a kid with a knife at one point. As an adult, I've made bad choices with some of my cases, and one boy is dead because of it. Another is in juvie. I didn't do my job today. Instead of babysitting Wyatt, I was on the phone getting interviewed for a job I'm not qualified for."

"Is that what you think?" Mom slowly shook her head. "You weren't kicked out of any foster homes. The first one was always meant as a temporary solution. The second one's parents had life circumstances they couldn't control, and they wanted better for you. The third family was prosecuted for abusing the kids. The fourth led us to you. You were no more rotten than any other kid out there. I don't care if you threatened anyone with a knife. Because I know you. Deep down, I know you. And that girl must have had a good reason to do it."

Emotion swelled in her chest. "But, Mom—"

"No, you're not going to convince me, Lauren. Nice try. You weren't responsible for that boy's death any more than you were responsible for Wyatt running off today. Look, these kids are doing things out of desperation, the same way you must have done."

Lauren knew that desperation. Had known it as a little girl. Still knew it now.

"Your dad and I are proud of you for wanting to help children, but don't ever think you're required to. If it's too hard, get into another field. God didn't put you on earth to save every soul you come into contact with. He's the one in the saving business. Let Him do His job."

Is that what she'd been trying to do? Save everyone?

Yes.

Her mom was right. She almost laughed at her arrogance. Who did she think she was?

Mom took her by the shoulders and stared into her eyes. "Lauren, you do understand God loves you as is, right? You can't earn His love. It's a grace thing."

That sobered her up. *A grace thing.*

"I've never let anyone get too close," Lauren said softly. "I don't even think I've let God get too close."

"It's never too late." Mom held her arms open. Lauren embraced her, inhaling the rose scent of her mother's favorite soap.

"I think I'm in love with Drew Gannon."

Mom stepped back, her mouth dropping open. "It's about time."

Lauren did a double take. "What do you mean by that?"

"I've waited years and years for you to get serious with someone. I'm ready for grandbabies to spoil."

Grandbabies?

"Don't get your hopes up. I was pretty awful to him this afternoon."

"You're a strong woman. Go there and apologize."

"I can't."

"You can."

"No, I mean, it's over. An apology isn't going to cut it." She'd burned her bridges. She was good at it. Had kept herself an island most of her life.

"He's a good man. He stares at you like you're a princess. He's strong, kind, and he works hard. Go after him."

That was the problem. He was good and kind and stared at her like she was something more than she could claim.

"If God loves you exactly the way you are, and your dad and I certainly do, don't you think Drew does, too?"

Lauren squeezed her eyes shut. It had taken time, but she'd grown to accept and cherish her parents' unconditional love. But Drew? He had feelings for her, sure. But he didn't love her.

If God loved her exactly as she was and her parents did the same, why didn't she love herself, flaws and all? Was it even possible?

She had enough to think about right now, and all she wanted to do was go home, crawl into bed and pretend today had never happened.

Chapter Thirteen

Drew held a paper plate with two slices of pepperoni pizza. Wyatt held an identical plate. They sat side by side in chairs on the backyard deck. Neither had touched their food or said a word since Drew picked him up from the Pierces'. He didn't know what to say. His anger had dissipated. Confusion had taken its place.

He was used to running these situations by Lauren to find out what to do. But this time he was on his own. He couldn't ask her how to handle the aftermath of Wyatt sneaking out. Not now. Not after all he'd said to her earlier.

He'd pushed her too far.

Right when he'd needed her the most.

He loved her, and this was his punishment for all the things he'd done wrong over the years. He'd fallen in love with beautiful-inside-and-out Lauren Pierce, and she was leaving.

And his promise?

Might be the one promise he shouldn't or couldn't keep. He'd told her he'd always be there for her, that nothing she did could ever push him away, but he wasn't what she needed. He took and took, and what did he give back?

He'd pressed her into a babysitting job she didn't want to take. Today, he'd saddled her with a tense situation beyond her control. Why hadn't he taken a leave of absence after the *People* magazine article came out? He'd seen the signs in Wyatt, too. The secrets. The attitude. And he'd ignored them, carrying on as if nothing was wrong. It had been easier than facing the truth.

"Uncle Drew?" Wyatt still hadn't touched his pizza. His eyes darted back and forth like a scared rabbit's.

"What, Wyatt?"

"What's going to happen now? Are you going to send me away?"

Send him away? Why would the kid ever think that?

"No. I would never send you away."

"You promise?"

Drew waved his fingers between Wyatt's eyes and his own. "You and I are family. There's nothing you can do to make me send you away. Got it?"

"It's just—"

"I know. You feel bad. You should feel bad. That's your conscience telling you that you messed up. But God forgives all sins—so pray for forgiveness and move on. Don't think it means you aren't going to have consequences, though."

"I'm sorry. I'm really sorry, Uncle Drew." He hiccupped, and sobs shook his slim body.

"Hey, it's okay." Drew put his arm around his shoulders. "I forgive you. I did a lot of dumb stuff when I was your age."

Wyatt wiped his eyes, and Drew gestured for him to stand. He set Wyatt on his lap, not caring if he was too old. "The important thing is you learn from your mistakes."

"You made mistakes?"

"I did. Still do." He held Wyatt tightly.

"Like what?"

"Oh, all kinds of things. Mostly little things I knew better than to do. You know, like cutting in line, cheating on a test, being mean to the captain of the cheerleading squad. I learned the hard way to do the right thing, though, and you will, too. Later on, we're going to sit down and hash out some rules."

"Okay."

"But first I want you to tell me why you snuck around to go play football. Do you want to play that badly?"

Wyatt stiffened, then exhaled. "Some of my friends think it's cool Dad played football. They told me they wanted me to be on their football team. I told them no, but they kept asking, and when I didn't say yes, they stopped talking to me."

"It is cool your dad played pro football. But you're cool, too. You don't need a superstar father to be someone worth hanging out with."

"After the magazine came out, one of them said I couldn't play because my dad was a jailbird."

Drew shifted his jaw. Why were kids so cruel?

"And I told him I could do whatever I wanted."

"So you did." Wyatt's actions made more sense now that Drew knew the backstory.

Wyatt nodded. "I miss Dad."

"I do, too."

"Uncle Drew, can I tell you something, and will you promise not to get mad?"

He hated promises like that, but he nodded.

"I used to think Dad had to go after Len, but I don't

think he had to at all. What about me? Why didn't he think about me?" He covered his face with his hands and cried. Drew rubbed his back, emotions pressing against his chest. This was one promise easy to keep.

"That's normal, buddy. I'm mad at him, too. I kept excusing him, telling myself what a great friend he's been—and he is a good friend, my best friend—but I didn't want to admit how much I miss him. How I wish he would have thought about you and me before he did it."

"Me, too."

"I think we need to forgive him. Both of us. He's a good man. He's still your dad. Still my best friend. He made a mistake, and he knows it. We're going to be okay until he gets out."

He lifted his head, his eyes swimming in tears. "I want to visit him again."

"It will be a little easier next time. We'll be ready for the pat down." Drew grinned and pretended to pat Wyatt's sides. He laughed. "And, listen, if you really, truly want to play football, I will talk to your dad about it."

Wyatt twisted his lips, considering. "I think I want to try soccer with Hunter."

"I'll sign you up tomorrow."

Wyatt hopped off his lap and returned to his seat. He took a big bite of his slice. After he'd chewed it, he said, "I shouldn't have gone today. I'm sorry. Think Lauren will forgive me?"

"She's just glad you're okay. But you still need to apologize to her. No bike riding unless it's with me, and I'm taking your iPod for two weeks."

"Two weeks?" he wailed.

"Want to make it three?"

Wyatt's lips lifted into a shy smile. "Two's fair."

They ate their pizza in the peace of the summer night. Maybe he wasn't so bad at raising Wyatt. Maybe he didn't need anyone's help.

He might not need it, but he wanted it. Lauren made everything easier. She was the part of him that had been missing his whole life.

And he'd blown it.

Lauren unlocked her apartment after leaving her parents' house and switched on the lights. She felt like she'd been hit by a truck. She idly browsed the stack of mail in her hands as she kicked the door shut behind her. Catalog, bill, advertising postcard. Tempted to dump it all in the trash, she moved the bill to the top of the pile and almost missed the letter underneath.

Treyvon.

Her breathing hitched. She stared at the plain white envelope for a long time. Then she went to the couch, curled her legs underneath her body and opened it. Unfolding the sheet, she paused. *Lord, whatever this letter contains, help me. Just help me read it.*

Neat handwriting and meticulous margins greeted her. Treyvon's teacher hadn't been kidding when she said he was a good student.

Miss Pierce,
I got your letter. If I would have gotten it a week earlier, I would have wadded it up and thrown it in the trash, but things happened I can't explain. You say you believe in God. I did, too, but after Jay died, I stopped believing. I had nothing left to live for.

Two days before your letter came, a pastor

made his weekly visit. I ignored that guy. God ignored me all my life. But something happened this time. The words the pastor said broke through. I finally understood the difference between believing there was a God and trusting in Jesus as my Savior. You probably think I'm crazy. Maybe I am. Anyway, after talking to the pastor, I prayed for a reason not to give up. When I opened your letter, I was sure you were going to tell me I was stupid and killed Jay. I know I'm the reason he died. He was trying to stop me. They told me they'd kill him if I didn't rob the store, but they killed him anyhow. I'll always live with that.

I was scared to open your letter, but hearing about the stuff you went through gave me hope. Thank you for writing. I hope you do it again.
Treyvon Smith

She folded the letter and slipped it back inside the envelope, pondering his words.

She'd poured her heart into the one she'd sent him. Told him about feeling unwanted. Shuffled off from home to home. Pulling the knife on that kid. How she still struggled to know her place in the world. She'd told him she wanted him to know he wasn't alone. That she cared about him. She'd asked him for forgiveness, for not helping them in time.

There were no coincidences. Three weeks ago she wouldn't have written the letter. She would have clung to her guilt, her need to blame Treyvon to assuage that guilt and her self-pity about the situation. She would not have reached out to him.

Three weeks ago, if she *would* have reached out to

him, he would have thrown her letter in the trash, and she would have assumed he blamed her, never to write him again.

God, You worked in my heart at just the right time. And You worked in Treyvon's heart at the right time. You sent the pastor when Treyvon was ready to hear the words. Oh, God, You truly are awesome! How did You take a preppy girl from sleepy Lake Endwell and an impoverished teen from a gang area and unite us in spirit? How did You change my heart? How did You change his?

The pastor. The Bible. Prayer. Her parents. Drew. All worked together to begin healing them.

Her mom had said something she'd been trying to ignore, but it grew louder in her mind until it drowned out her other thoughts.

God didn't put you on earth to save every soul you come into contact with. He's in the saving business. Let Him do His job.

It really *was* a grace thing.

Tears sprung to her eyes, falling down her cheeks in little rivers. *Thank You, Jesus!*

The burden she'd been carrying vanished. She felt free. Free! She smiled through her tears. Wanted to jump in the air. Why not? She got to her feet, pumped her hands in the air and did a tuck. Laughed as she landed. Boy, she needed to stretch before she attempted that again.

She didn't deserve forgiveness, this apartment, her health, her parents, Wyatt, Drew—anything! She never had deserved them. Never would! But God gave them to her because He loved her.

He loves me.

She sobered up at the word *love*. She loved Drew. And she'd thrown him out. Literally kicked him out of her apartment. She'd driven him away.

Out of fear.

Out of shame.

Out of guilt.

He'd made her a promise, and she'd told him she was letting him out of it. Had she driven him away for good?

She would have to apologize. Beg. Get on her knees if necessary. But she had to tell him how she felt—how she really felt.

Drew had to be mad at her. She didn't want to tell him she loved him in front of Wyatt if things got heated. The kid didn't need more drama in his overly dramatic life. And, frankly, she'd been so awful earlier, a simple apology and "By the way, I love you," weren't going to cut it.

How could she get Drew alone?

An idea formed. A wonderful, scary idea.

God, give me the courage.

Drew dangled his legs off the edge of the dock and into the warm lake. Stars blinked overhead, and a crescent moon reflected off the water. He'd tucked Wyatt in an hour ago, and after tidying the living room and trying to avoid the tangled web of thoughts in his head, he gave up and came out here. What was he going to do about Lauren?

He'd told Wyatt earlier he'd done a lot of dumb things as a kid. He'd done them as an adult, too. And God had forgiven every stupid thing he'd done.

Had Drew really done anything that dumb with Lauren? So he'd pushed her. He'd probably do the same again. It drove him nuts she was missing all the great parts of herself by focusing on what she perceived as her failures.

Kind of like I've done since I moved back here.

Lauren was kind, generous, strong, courageous and compassionate. She had a lot of great parts to focus on. Unlike him.

Says who?

Why was he still defining himself by his past?

He was doing a decent job raising Wyatt. His co-workers were accepting him. So he'd acted like a jerk in high school. He'd outgrown that. And big deal he'd gotten kicked out of college. He'd been blessed with a career doing something he loved.

Were he and Lauren doing the same thing? Clinging to regrets for no reason?

Her early years had done a number on her. He frowned, thinking of the things she'd told him. She probably hadn't felt worth loving.

Did she still not feel worth loving?

Didn't he feel the same? Was *he* worth loving?

Leaning back, he rested his hands on the deck. If he'd learned anything from his mistakes, he'd learned not to give up on himself.

He didn't want to give up on this. On her, on them, on what they could be.

If he was really the man he thought he was, he wouldn't give up because she told him to leave during an emotional meltdown. That would be like not showing up to those team meetings in college. Or getting halfway into a burning building and calling it quits.

He'd been trained to see things through.

She was worth fighting for. He wasn't giving up on her. Not now. Not tomorrow. Not next year.

Whatever it took, however long it took, he would fight for her.

Chapter Fourteen

"What would I do without you, Megan?" Lauren lugged the stack of doughnut boxes from the trunk of her car. Closing it, she took a deep breath. "Thank you. Thank you so much."

"Are you kidding me? I feel like we're on a secret mission. For love! Aah!" Megan clapped her hands, her eyes shining. "Don't worry. Ben and Tony will get Drew and Wyatt to the station. And then you can whisk Drew away, and we'll take care of Wyatt." Megan gave her a knowing stare. "For as long as it takes."

Lauren walked toward the station door. "It might not take long. I was obnoxious yesterday. I can't believe how rude I was."

Megan waved her hand as if her words meant nothing. "We all say stupid stuff when we're upset. He'll get over it. He probably already has."

Maybe. Maybe not. "Thanks for all your help with this. You're brilliant."

"I'm glad you asked me! Oh, look at the time—we'd better get in there."

"I'm nervous. He's going to reject me. I can feel it."

"That's your nerves talking."

"But what if—"

Megan placed her hand on Lauren's arm. "Calm down. If it doesn't work out, I have the whole day off, and we'll get through it. Together. But you don't have to worry. He likes you."

Likes? Or loves? There was a big difference.

They arrived at the doorway too soon. Maybe she should leave. She hadn't had time to talk herself out of this, and the more she thought about it, the more she felt like she was going to throw up.

Telling Drew she loved him? Asking his forgiveness? *Bad idea.*

Bad.

But Megan had already gone inside, and Tony was holding the door open.

Lord, I can't do this. I'm a coward! My parents chose me, but I've never chosen anyone. I've been too afraid all this time. How can I do it now?

Tony frowned, letting the door close behind him. "You okay?"

"I don't know." She shook her head.

"I'm impressed you've helped Drew out with Wyatt all this time. And, hey, it's nice of you to bring all these doughnuts. Don't worry, I called him this morning. Three times. They're on their way."

Her nerves settled the tiniest bit. She didn't make a habit of sharing her feelings with anyone, but she was desperate. "Tony?"

"What?"

"He's pretty great, isn't he?"

Tony grinned and patted her shoulder. "He is. Why don't you collect your thoughts out here, and I'll make sure Ben and Megan aren't getting too cozy inside."

She let out a nervous laugh and sat on the bench near

the door. Chewed on a fingernail as she crossed one leg over the other, kicking nervously. Her stomach couldn't be any more rowdy. It was as if the national cheerleading competition was taking place in there.

What if this didn't work? What if he never wanted to see her again? What if...

"Lauren?" Drew approached her with Wyatt next to him. "What are you doing here?"

"I had to talk to you. To both of you." She rose, holding her arms open to Wyatt, hugging him tightly for a long time.

"I'm sorry, Lauren," Wyatt said. "I didn't mean to scare you yesterday. I feel really bad."

She pressed her lips to his soft hair. "I forgive you. I'm so thankful you're safe." She stepped back, peering into his eyes. "You scared me to death, though. Don't you know how important you are to me?"

Wyatt blinked rapidly. "I guess I do now."

"Well, don't forget it. I love you, Wyatt. Don't ever scare me like that again."

He grinned. "I won't."

"Come on—let's go inside. Megan and I brought doughnuts for everyone. We wanted to thank them for helping us find you." Wyatt opened the door, and Lauren put her hand on Drew's arm. "Can we talk in a little bit?"

His face was unreadable. "Sure."

She wished she could decipher his tone. They went inside to the kitchen. Everyone was munching on doughnuts, laughing and sipping juice or coffee. Ben put his arm around Wyatt's neck and was pretending to rub his head. Wyatt laughed.

"Thanks for helping us out yesterday." Drew pulled Tony into a half embrace.

She couldn't help thinking Tony and Drew had more in common than they realized. Now if she could just get Drew to view *her* differently...

"No problem, man. Um, I think someone wants to talk to you." Tony widened his eyes, nodding at Lauren.

Drew rubbed the back of his neck. "Will you guys watch Wyatt for a minute?"

Megan scooted to his side. "Ben and I want to take Wyatt for a pontoon ride later. Would that be okay with you?"

"Let me ask Wyatt."

While Drew discussed the plan with Wyatt, Lauren pulled Megan to her side and whispered, "I can't do this. I'm going to hurl."

"You can do it," she whispered back. "You walked the streets of Chicago. You're tough."

"But that was just drug dealers and gangs. This is Drew."

"Go." Megan took her by the shoulders, turned her and marched her down the hall to the garage, where the fire trucks and ambulances were parked. "I'll send him out there."

The garage doors were open, letting in the brilliant sunlight. Lauren walked on shaky legs to the ladder truck and sat on the front bumper.

And when she looked up, Drew stood in front of her, legs wide, arms crossed over his buff chest. The man was dangerously good-looking. And his personality clinched the deal. Her heart did a double back handspring. She rose. Swallowed.

"I'm sorry." She forced herself to look into his eyes. They didn't seem to hate her. "I'm sorry I threw you out. I'm sorry I acted like your promise meant nothing to me. It wasn't nothing. It's not nothing. Besides the day my parents told me they were adopting me, it was the best thing I've ever heard."

Drew's mouth had opened while she spoke, but she didn't give him a chance to respond.

"I kind of flipped out yesterday. Like everything that had been building inside me my entire life snapped. I never realized I was trying to make up for my early childhood by being perfect. Mom told me some stuff that hit home with me. And I wanted to believe it, but I couldn't let myself."

Drew inched closer. The muscle in his cheek flexed.

"I got a letter from Treyvon. It helped open my eyes to reality. I've thought I had to be in control all this time, making the right choices, helping anyone I could, but I had it all wrong. God is in control. He's led me to situations where I could help, but ultimately, it wasn't up to me."

Drew moved closer. So close she could smell his aftershave and see the pulse in his throat. "Lauren—"

"I'm not done." She looked up into his eyes, took a deep breath. "You're right. We have choices. And I chose to push you away, but I don't want to anymore. I'm grateful for you. You don't let anything stop you from achieving your goals. I'm amazed at how good you are with Wyatt. I'm dumbfounded you're so good to me. I don't deserve it."

Drew hauled her to him, the warmth of his chest seeping into hers, and claimed her lips. She had more to say, but his arms surrounded her, protecting her, cherishing her, and she forgot the rest of her speech. None of it mattered, anyhow. She kissed him back.

"Drew, thank you for believing in me, for allowing me to get close to you and Wyatt. You made me a promise, and now I'm making one of my own. No matter how messy or difficult life gets, I won't run away. Because I love you."

"Are you about done, woman?" With his forehead against hers, Drew stared into her eyes, keeping his arms locked around her waist.

Lauren Pierce had just told him she loved him.

It seemed inconceivable. For years, he'd had to fight for everything he wanted. He'd fully expected to wake up and fight for her today. Two dozen pink roses sat in his truck. When Tony had called this morning, he'd refused to come to the station, but by the third call, he'd given up. Decided when he got here, he'd ask someone to watch Wyatt for an hour while he tried to convince Lauren they were right for each other.

The magnitude of God's blessing filled him with wonder.

He held her hands. "There is nothing to forgive. I knew you were upset yesterday, and I shouldn't have pushed you."

"Yes, you should have. I needed it. You were right about all of us having choices."

"I went home last night and had a long talk with Wyatt. He knows he made the wrong one. I think part of him did it to get back at Chase, if that makes sense. And the other part wanted to impress some kids."

"It does make sense. Those bruised and bloody parts inside us make us do things we know aren't smart. I should know."

"I know, too. I've been stuck in regrets. You helped me see I've changed. Before I moved here, I'd been hiding from my past. Let's face it—I avoided Lake Endwell for more than a decade. But you didn't see me the way

I saw myself. And if anyone should have, it was you. Lauren Pierce, I love you."

"You do? But I—"

"Yes, I love you. I couldn't love you more than I do right here, right now. I'll get on the speaker system and announce it to the entire fire station if I have to, but I want you to be one hundred percent certain of this—I love you, and I'm never giving up on you."

Tears slipped down her cheeks. "You really love me? I didn't think you could—"

He silenced her with his lips. He couldn't believe his dream girl was in his arms. Genuine—Lauren was genuine.

With a contented sigh, she pulled away. "If you change your mind—"

"Will you be quiet for one minute?" he asked. She blinked. "I've loved you for a while, but I didn't want to admit it."

She grinned, tracing his cheek with her finger. "Same here. So you're not mad? I don't have to get on my knees and beg?"

The only way to get her to stop talking seemed to be kissing her. He pressed his lips to hers again. She tasted like forever.

Reluctantly, he ended the kiss. "You made me see I'm capable of more than I thought. I was clueless about raising Wyatt through all this drama before you had mercy on us. You've given me confidence. Not just in being Wyatt's father, but in myself in general. I don't know how I got so blessed to have you, but I'm not letting you go. Ever."

"Good. I don't want you to let me go. Ever."

He got lost in her eyes, smiling in understanding.

"So yesterday you said you were withdrawing your application to be the high school counselor."

She shook her head. "Not anymore. I think for the first time in my life I'm truly prepared to help emotionally damaged kids. It's not all on my shoulders anymore. It's on God's."

"Smart woman." He loved the way she felt in his arms. "Do you still want to babysit Wyatt? You don't have to. I can find someone else if it's too much."

"I want to. I've always wanted to. I love Wyatt, and the thought of losing him scared me so much." She stood on her tiptoes and kissed him, then added, "Do you still want me to babysit?"

"I clearly haven't convinced you." He claimed her lips, but the sound of applause made him lift his head. *What in the world?*

Everyone who'd been in the kitchen stood in the garage and whooped and hollered.

Wyatt ran to Drew, and he scooped the kid into his arms. "So, buddy, I kind of fell in love with your babysitter."

"She's really pretty, Uncle Drew." He smiled, all teeth, up at Lauren. She laughed.

"She sure is."

"I have a confession, too, Wyatt. I kind of fell in love with your uncle."

"Well, he is a firefighter." Wyatt made it sound as if that explained everything.

"He sure is."

"Are you two going to get married?"

A hush fell over everyone.

Drew glanced at Lauren, her eyes shining bright, and he smiled. "Let's take it one day at a time, okay?"

"Hey, Wyatt," Megan said. "Let's let the two love-birds have some privacy. We'll go out on the lake."

"Yes!" Wyatt pumped his fist in the air. "Can I drive the pontoon?"

"You're way too young." Ben put his arm around Wyatt's shoulders, leading him away.

Drew took Lauren's hand and dragged her out of there to where his truck was parked. He pulled the bouquet out of the backseat and handed it to her. "I was on my way over to convince you to give us a chance."

"Too late. I'm convinced." She lifted the pink roses to her nose, beaming, and inhaled their scent. "All these beautiful flowers for me?"

He wrapped her up in his arms. "Everything for you. That's a promise."

Epilogue

❧

"Stop fidgeting."

"I can't help it." Drew clasped his hands as he stood next to Tony at the front of the church. Today was the day. Lauren Pierce would soon be Lauren Gannon. *Thank You, Lord.*

They'd dated all summer, and he'd asked her to marry him at halftime during the homecoming football game at Lake Endwell High. Her cheerleading squad had helped him plan it. All he'd known was she'd said yes. And now here it was, almost Christmas, and he couldn't be happier. Or more nervous.

He glanced over at Wyatt at the end of the line of his groomsmen. Wyatt gave him a thumbs-up. Drew winked back. He wished Chase could be there, but it would be a few more years before he'd be out of prison. Surprisingly, Chase had started writing Treyvon after Drew had mentioned the kid's situation. Chase had become Treyvon's mentor and planned on working with at-risk youth when he was released.

The prewedding music stopped, and everyone stood. Drew's breath caught at the sight of Lauren. The organ began playing as Lauren walked up the aisle on her father's arm. Drew hadn't thought she could be more beautiful, but today she positively glowed. Her white gown had short cap sleeves, lace overlays and intricate beading. It showed off her slim waist, and her hair was piled on top of her head. She carried a bouquet of pink roses. After handing the bouquet to Megan, her maid of honor, she hugged her dad, and he placed her arm on Drew's.

Sweat broke out on his forehead, but he didn't dare wipe it away. He glanced her way, and she smiled. That smile did something to him. His nerves fled. Joy filled his heart. He tucked her hand more closely under his arm. His to protect. To cherish.

"Do you take this man to be your husband?"

"I do."

He slid the ring on her finger, meeting her gaze, promising her forever with his eyes.

She was really his.

The service went by in a flash. Drew and Lauren strolled down the aisle together, and before the bridesmaids and groomsmen joined them, he dragged her to the side.

"Lauren?"

"Yes?" Her teeth sparkled she was smiling so wide.

"We're married."

"I know." She scrunched her nose, sounding awed.

He claimed her lips, holding her close. He couldn't believe he was privileged enough to spend the rest of his life with this amazing woman.

"Okay, okay, break it up, you two." Tony clapped him on the shoulder. The bridesmaids and groomsmen formed a circle around them. "We have a little surprise for you. It's a tradition."

Chief Reynolds popped his head into the group. "For the record, I know nothing about this." He waved and left.

"You're coming with us." Tony grinned.

Lauren elbowed Drew. "Do you know anything about this?"

"Not a clue." But he could guess.

"Everybody to the station."

A gentle snow fell as they stepped outside, and Lauren laughed, still carrying her bouquet.

"Are you cold? Take my jacket." He shrugged off his tuxedo jacket and draped it over her shoulders. He slipped his arm around her waist and lifted her off her feet, carrying her the short distance to his truck, which had been decorated with balloons and a "Just Married" sign.

"Did you do this?" Lauren asked.

"Nope."

They stared at each other a minute in the truck and burst out laughing.

"This is fun," she said. "No one told me getting married was fun."

"It is. Getting married to *you* is fun." He leaned across the seat and kissed her.

A few minutes later they pulled up to the fire station. The garage doors stood open, and the bridal party and everyone on duty had lined up by one of the trucks.

"Do I even want to know?" Lauren asked. Drew grabbed her hand and they ran inside.

"Attention, everyone." Tony raised his hands. "Our own Gannon the Cannon got married today. You know what this means."

They all solemnly nodded.

"Drew, if you want the marriage to last, you need to kiss her on the fire truck."

One of the guys whooped.

"I'll kiss her for you, Drew," another hollered.

"Not on your life, Miggs," Drew shot back. Laughter erupted.

Tony brought Drew's helmet over and handed it to Lauren. "Sorry, sweetheart, but this might mess up your hair."

"So it guarantees a lasting marriage?" She pretended to consider it. "I'll take messed-up hair."

She set the helmet on her head, and Drew climbed onto the side of the truck. He held his hand out and hauled her up. Her body brushed his.

"Go on already, Gannon. Kiss the girl!"

He grinned, not taking his eyes off Lauren.

And he kissed her.

"How was that?" he asked.

She glanced up sideways and bit her lip. "Umm…"

His kiss wasn't up to her standards? He'd show her. This time he captured her lips, luxuriating in her touch, and he didn't let up.

"Whoa, there. Get a room, you two!"

He stepped down and held his arms wide. She jumped into them.

"I have everything I'll ever need right here in my arms," he whispered into her ear.

"You're all I'll ever need. I love you, Drew."

"I love you, too, Mrs. Gannon. Forever. I will never let you go."

* * * * *

If you enjoyed Drew and Lauren's story,
pick up Jill Kemerer's other books
set in Lake Endwell:

SMALL-TOWN BACHELOR
UNEXPECTED FAMILY
HER SMALL-TOWN ROMANCE
YULETIDE REDEMPTION

Available now from Love Inspired!
Find more great reads at www.LoveInspired.com

Dear Reader,

I'm fascinated by the life choices people make, and I admire individuals like Lauren and Drew, who chose professions requiring sacrifice. They each overcame difficult pasts to dedicate their lives to helping others. Lauren dealt with the heartbreaking reality of kids with few options, forced to choose between bad and worse. Although my life is far from the poverty and crime of the inner city, my heart goes out to anyone trapped in desperate circumstances. One thing I know—we all need a helping hand, a kind word, someone believing in us. May we all try to see the people around us through God's eyes, the eyes of love.

I love connecting with readers. You can learn more at www.jillkemerer.com and email me at jill@jillkemerer.com.

God bless you!
Jill Kemerer

COMING NEXT MONTH FROM
Love Inspired®

Available June 20, 2017

A SECRET AMISH LOVE
Women of Lancaster County • by Rebecca Kertz

With her father insisting she marry, Nell Stoltzfus is feeling the pressure to figure out her future. A decision that is further complicated when she falls for English veterinarian James Pierce. Dare she risk being shunned to be with the man her heart has claimed as its own?

THE COWBOY'S BABY BLESSING
Cowboy Country • by Deb Kastner

Cowboy Seth Howell's adventure-seeking days suddenly change when he inherits custody of his two-year-old godson. With day-care owner Rachel Perez by his side, teaching him how to care for little Caden, he'll learn that family is the greatest adventure of all.

HER COWBOY BOSS
The Prodigal Ranch • by Arlene James

Stark Burns and Meri Billings are like oil and water—so he's shocked when she asks for a position in his veterinary clinic. For Meri, it's her only option if she wants to stay close to home and family. Soon their differences fall away as Meri teaches the widower how to live—and love—again.

THE TWINS' FAMILY WISH
Wranglers Ranch • by Lois Richer

Finding someone to watch his orphaned twin niece and nephew is Rick Granger's priority—and he thinks teacher Penny Stern is just the person. Before long, he offers Penny a marriage of convenience for the children's sake—but will their pretend union turn into the future they both always wished for?

DEPUTY DADDY
Comfort Creek Lawmen • by Patricia Johns

Diaper duty was the last thing officer Bryce Camden expected during his stay in Comfort Creek. But with lovely Lily Ellison, owner of the B and B where he's staying, asking for his help with her foster baby, he'll soon be more than a bachelor cop—he'll be a family man.

CHILD WANTED
Willow's Haven • by Renee Andrews

Proven innocent of a crime she was unjustly accused of, Lindy Burnett desperately wants to regain her parental rights. Ethan Green is determined to adopt Lindy's son and protect him from harm. Can coming to an agreement about little Jerry also lead to an agreement to spend their lifetime together?

LOOK FOR THESE AND OTHER LOVE INSPIRED BOOKS WHEREVER BOOKS ARE SOLD, INCLUDING MOST BOOKSTORES, SUPERMARKETS, DISCOUNT STORES AND DRUGSTORES.

LICNM0617

"You said your *bruder* was called out on an emergency," Nell said. "What does he do?"

"He's a veterinarian. He's recently opened a clinic here in Happiness."

The strange sensation settled over Nell. Despite the difference in their last names, could James be Maggie's brother? "What's his name?" she asked.

"James Pierce." Maggie smiled. "He owns Pierce Veterinary Clinic. Have you heard of him?"

"*Ja.* In fact, 'twas your bruder who treated my dog, Jonas."

"Then you've met him!" Maggie looked delighted. "Is he a *gut* veterinarian?"

Startled by this new knowledge, Nell could only nod at first. "He was wonderful with Jonas. He's a kind and compassionate man." She studied Maggie and recognized the family resemblance. "How is he a Pierce and you a Troyer?"

"I am a Pierce." Maggie grinned. "Abigail is, too. But we don't go by the Pierce name. Adam is our stepfather, and he is our *dat* now." Maggie's eyes filled with sadness. "I was too young to care, but James had a hard time with it. He loved Dad, and he'd wanted to be a veterinarian like him since he was ten. He became more determined to follow in Dad's footsteps."

Nell felt her heart break for James, who must have suffered after his father's death. "You chose the Amish life, but James chose a different path."

"And he's doing well," Maggie said. "My family is thrilled that he set up his practice in Happiness."

Later that afternoon, James arrived to spend time with his family.

She recognized his car immediately as he drove into the barnyard. James stood a moment, searching for family members. Nell couldn't move as he crossed the yard to where tables and bench seats had been set up. Soon, James headed to the gathering of young people, including his sisters Maggie and Abigail.

Nell found it heartwarming to see that his siblings regarded him with the same depth of love and affection. James spoke briefly to Maggie, clearly delighted that he'd handled his emergency then decided to come. She heard the siblings teasing and the ensuing laughter. Maggie said something to James as she gestured in Nell's direction.

James saw her, and Nell froze. Her heart started to beat hard when he broke away from the group to approach her.

Don't miss
A SECRET AMISH LOVE
by Rebecca Kertz, available July 2017 wherever
Love Inspired® books and ebooks are sold.

www.LoveInspired.com